Don't Call at All

Robbie Myles

Copyright © 2020 by Robbie Myles

Cover Art – Cameron Roubique, 2020

All rights reserved, including the right to reproduce this book or portions thereof in any form whatsoever.

This book is a work of fiction. Any references to historical events, real people, or real places are used fictitiously. Other names, characters, places and events are products of the author's imagination, and any resemblance to actual events or places or persons, living or dead, is entirely coincidental.

ISBN 9798578940279

This book is for
Judy, Eric, Maxi, Zenda and Kanter.

Chapter 1

Hi, I'm Jessie Davidson, and boy, do I have a story for you. It all started with a big fight between my parents and me.

"You're just not old enough, Jess!" Mom shouted at me. Dad was also in the kitchen, waiting to give his two cents.

"I hate to say it, squirt, but Mom's got a point. You're only thirteen. Those things will turn your brain to mush!" Dad said.

"But Mom, Dad, every kid at school has one. Please? I'll never ask you for anything else ever again, I swear."

Of course, I didn't actually mean that. But I needed to tell them something legit if I wanted to make a real case. I was usually pretty solid with the guilt trip routine. My puppy dog face was epic. "You don't want me to be the only kid without a phone, do you? I'll be a total loser! Even Marcus Sneadleman just got one!"

Marcus was the biggest weenie in school. He was short, super nerdy, had huge, thick red glasses, and never showered.

"Oh, well, in that case, I suppose we should just spend five hundred dollars and get you your precious device, shouldn't we?" Mom's tone was sarcastic.

"Why do you care what Marcus Sneadleman does, squirt? What does it matter if he's got a phone and you don't?"

I hated when Dad did this. He always tried to be the voice of reason. But it wouldn't work this time, Dad. Not this time. I refused to be the only kid at school without a cell phone!

"This is about *you*, squirt! Don't conform to societal expectations; don't give in to peer pressure. Besides, what does a thirteen-year-old need a cell phone for, anyway?" Dad said.

The truth was that I didn't *need* a cell phone, but I truly, badly, desperately *wanted* one. Last year, all my friends had started getting phones, and they were the coolest things to have. Everyone made their own Instagram accounts, and if you didn't have one, you were totally left out of every inside joke and popular topic of conversation.

Just this past week, I had walked up to Josh Hartley and Nelson Strong to say what's up. The two of them had been in my class since we were five. I gave them a nod and tried to have a conversation. Neither of them looked up from their phones for even one second, and then they both started laughing.

"What's so funny?" I asked.

"Check your Insta, Jessie!" I was immediately crushed. I didn't have an Insta, since I didn't have a phone.

I responded, "Oh, cool, yeah, I'll do that later."

The two of them walked away, still looking down at their phones. I found out later that there was some meme all the eighth graders were laughing at. It was all the rage. In short, having a phone meant having a social life. I had to have one.

I got down on my knees. "Please, Mom. Please, Dad, I kneel here before you as your only son, your precious baby. This is a life-or-death situation. I must have this phone. This is not a drill. This is not a joke. Please and thank you." I was quite convincing, I must say.

I usually didn't ask for much. I was a good kid, always got As and Bs, and for the most part, my parents got me the things I wanted. But on the phone issue, they would not budge. They were a brick wall of no. And it didn't seem like that would change anytime soon.

Dad began talking, but Mom interrupted him. "Listen, buddy. We hear you, we really do. You know us. We want you to be happy and have the things you want, but this … this is just not something we can get behind. We don't want to get you a cell phone simply because everyone else has one. When we feel it's important for you to have one, we will get it for you, I promise."

I thought for a long time before responding. "What if I get abducted tomorrow by a band of nasty space aliens, and my only chance of survival is to call you from my cell phone to tell you my whereabouts?"

Mom and Dad looked at each other for a moment and sighed. "I think we'll take our chances, Jess." Clearly, they were losing interest in this whole conversation. I realized that my efforts were for nothing. They weren't budging, and no puppy dog face was going to change that.

I grunted and stormed out of the kitchen and into my bedroom. Buttons followed me, wagging his tail. Buttons was my little buddy. He was an adorable thirty-pound Golden Doodle that my parents had gotten me for my eighth birthday. He was the best. Although I loved him dearly and he was the best company ever, he couldn't help me with my current problem.

I jumped into bed, and Buttons followed behind me. He nudged his head and ears into the pocket of my armpit and nuzzled me. "I love you, too, Butts." He licked my face and rolled onto his back. All four of his legs stood up straight. I rubbed his belly.

"Jessie, come in. Jessie, do you copy? I repeat, do you copy?" *Brad*, I thought. I pushed Buttons over onto his stomach and leaned over to grab my walkie-talkie.

"This is Jessie. Copy."

"What's your status, buddy?"

"My status? You want to know my status? I am lying here alone in my room with my dog. Parents gave me a hard no on the cell phone."

"Brutal. Meet me outside in ten. Over." Brad said.

Brad was my best friend since second grade and lived two buildings down from me on 84th Street. We lived on the Upper East Side in New York City. We used to get together so often that our parents thought we needed a break from each other. That's why they got us the walkie-talkies. This way, we can be inseparable from our bedrooms.

The more I thought about cell phones, the more not having one haunted me! I simply couldn't believe I still didn't have one. What was I supposed to do?

My parents always said that the only person I really spoke to was Brad, and they were probably right. But at thirteen, my entire popularity status depended on my ability to keep up with the kids at school. Every eighth grader had a phone, and if you didn't, then you just didn't matter—it was as simple as that. If you weren't able to get in on group chats about the latest gossip or check out the newest viral video, you just couldn't hack it in a social circle.

I grabbed my jacket and threw it on over my favorite hoodie, laced up my winter boots, and put on a hat. "You coming, Butts?" I looked over at my sweet little Buttons. He didn't move a muscle.

I thumped down the stairs in my boots and greeted

my parents in the kitchen. Dad looked up from his paper. "Where are you off to, squirt?"

"Have a date with some aliens. This might be the end of me." If my parents thought I would give up so easily, they were mistaken.

"Have fun with Brad, squirt." Dad said.

"Be home by seven, and don't make us worry!" Mom said.

"No problem, I'll be sure to call from my cell phone!" I joked.

And on that note, I walked out of our apartment and headed down to meet Brad.

Chapter 2

Brad and I met in the same spot we always met, on the corner of 86th Street and 2nd Avenue. Before he even said hi to me, Brad was going off about social media.

"Dude, I got twenty-three likes this morning. Twenty-three! Not only that, but Sara Tompkins liked it," Brad said.

Brad had gotten his phone for his thirteenth birthday this past summer. He was on it constantly. It was like we'd gained a third best friend. I guess it wasn't so bad. At least Brad was able to keep me updated on what was happening on social media. Not like it mattered, though—by the time he showed me something or told me about it, I was way late to the party.

Having your own phone was what mattered. Last week, Brad had been invited to a group chat with, like, half of our eighth-grade class. A group chat that I wasn't a part of.

"Oh, and check this out, Jess Man!" Brad showed me a video on Instagram of Sara and all of her friends walking their dogs in the neighborhood.

"Well, isn't that great, Brad. It seems like you and Sara are bonding. Maybe one day, you'll actually talk in person," I said.

"In person? As in, face-to-face? But why? What's the point?" Brad said.

I doubted Brad would even know what to say if Sara Tompkins ever walked up to him in person and began talking.

We trudged down the snowy sidewalks on our normal route along 86th street and across to 5th avenue.

"Gentleman!" The voice spoke out to us from the food cart window. The smell of bacon, eggs, and coffee filled our nostrils.

"Yo, Geno!" Brad responded.

Geno owned the food cart a few blocks away from my apartment, and his food was the best. He always hooked us up for free if we didn't have money on us.

"We'll take the usual, Geno," I said. Geno disappeared to the back of his cart for a minute before returning with our food.

"You guys enjoy, and I'll catch you on the flip! Tomorrow, same time, same place." Geno fist-bumped us both, and with our sandwiches in hand, we began walking away.

We only made it a few steps before Geno called out to us. "Oh, dudes! I almost forgot to ask! Did you guys see the video of that guy juggling those dogs? Man, that was wild!"

I glanced at Brad, who knew exactly what I was thinking.

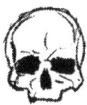

We kept walking along our usual route. "So they wouldn't budge, huh?" Brad asked me.

"Not one bit," I replied.

"Did you tell them your social life is reliant on getting a phone? Did you tell them that you are destined for a life of loser-ness, all because of them?" Brad carried on.

Like me, Brad couldn't believe that I still didn't have a phone. Everyone we knew in eighth grade had one. It was how we lived, how we went about our daily lives. It was a part of who we were.

"Yes, yes, and yes," I replied.

"Believe me, I tried everything, man. I really did. They just don't get it. When they were kids, no one had phones, so they have no idea what it's like. I wish I could somehow let them live in my shoes for a day. I want them to see what being a thirteen-year-old in 2019 feels like!"

I pictured my dad as a thirteen-year-old, sitting in front of a small television in his living room. I didn't know how he'd survived. I'd seen pictures of what he looked like when he was young, and it was eerily similar to how I look.

"Did you beg and plead?" Brad said.

"I tried everything, my dude. Believe me, if there was anything I could do—ANYTHING—you know I would've done it. I'm just doomed. This is it. I'll be left out of the social scene for the rest of my days."

I looked Brad in the eyes, then off into the distance before I continued. "You'll go on, and eventually Sara will start liking more and more of your photos. You'll start dating, leaving no time for me, of course," I said.

Brad was stuffing his face with eggs as I spoke.

"I understand if you just want to cut ties with me now. It will make it easier on me in the long run." I knew I was being dramatic, but I had to get my point across.

"Yeah, I suppose it's for the best." Bits of egg spittled out everywhere as Brad spoke.

"Dude, no way!" I hit Brad in the shoulder as I spoke, and we both laughed.

"Hey, what's going on over there?" Brad pointed across the street. There was a crowd of people gathered around something.

"I don't know, let's check it out," I said.

We walked closer to the crowd of people and saw something horrible. There was a man wearing a large brown robe that looked kinda like a Snuggie launching himself at people, cackling with laughter.

When we got in close, the man lifted his head into the air and let out a high-pitched shriek of a laugh. It wasn't until his hood came off that we saw the really terrifying thing. The man's hood had fallen off his head, and we both gasped at what was underneath.

The man was ghostly pale, and his skin had a greenish tint. There were lumps and moles that seemed to be eating away at him, patches of brown slime seeping over his face and head. The man also had the greenest eyes I had ever seen.

"That poor guy," Brad said.

I didn't respond. I kept my eyes on the man in the crowd. His skin was pulled tight across his bones. It looked like his whole body was slowly deteriorating, like pretty soon there would be nothing left of him, only a skeleton. There was something wrong with this man. He was not healthy.

"Maybe he's got the flu or something," Brad said.

"That's no flu. That man does not look good," I responded.

"Something just flew out of his mouth. I think I'm gonna be sick," Brad said as he turned his head in the other direction at the sight of the green gob of ooze that flung from the man's mouth.

As the man stood up and gained his composure, he looked directly at me, and kept his stare for what seemed like an eternity. I couldn't tell for sure, but it looked like a grin had slowly spread over his lips.

I couldn't look away, either. This man looked like something out of a horror movie. He looked grotesque, like a skeleton or zombie.

Our eyes were locked on each other's for what seemed like forever.

"Help me, Jessie," the man mouthed to me, and then his eyes moved elsewhere, and he lifted his arms uproariously into the air and yawped at the crowd of people as he scurried away.

"Dude, did you see that?" I was trembling.

"Yeah, super gross, man. That guy was straight out of a horror movie."

"No, did you see what he said to me?"

"Said to you? What do you mean?" Brad said.

"He just spoke to me. He mouthed something to me."

I was still in shock. The large crowd of people were in a furious boggle. No one could comprehend what had just happened.

What was happening to that man? Part of me wanted to follow him, as I was mesmerized. But the other part of me—the sane part of me—wanted to run and never speak of this again.

Brad looked at me, unnerved. "Wh-what did he say?"

"I think he said, 'Help me, Jessie.' I think he knew my name."

Chapter 3

"Maybe he's, like, your long-lost relative, Jess. Maybe he can buy you a cell phone!"

I punched Brad in the shoulder again for joking around about this.

"It's not funny, dude. That guy knew my name. I swear."

"Jessie, there is no way that guy knows who you are. You're just imagining it. Do you know who *he* is?" Brad asked.

"No," I replied.

"Then there ya go! If you don't know him, how can he possibly know you? And don't you think you would remember if you knew a guy who looked like that? Who looked like a living zombie?"

I supposed Brad was right. But that didn't change the fact that I was seriously weirded out. There was something majorly off about that man. It was more than his appearance. As soon as I saw him, I felt a darkness come over me. It was strange, to say the least.

I tried not to think about it as Brad and I continued walking over to the park. "Man, I can't wait to see everyone's reaction when I upload this!"

"Upload what?" I said.

"That. That whole thing! That was cray-cray!" Brad responded.

"You got that on video?" I said.

My first question was why Brad would ever want to see that again. Just thinking about the hideous, zombie skin and skeleton-like bones of that man gave me goose bumps. And I *definitely* didn't want Brad to share it with the world. It felt wrong to do.

"What's the point of uploading it? I think I might vomit just thinking about it," I said.

"Um, so that I can get some serious likes!" Brad said. "I bet you Sara will like it." Now he was smiling. "She loves scary things."

Within minutes of uploading the video, Brad had a ton of likes and comments. Sara did like it, of course. Someone even commented, "This guy for president!"

As badly as I wanted a phone, in that moment, I was glad I didn't have to stare at Brad's video on social media. Something felt very wrong about the whole thing. And did that man really know my name? It had to have been my imagination. I'd never seen him before in my life. I could never have forgotten someone who looked like that.

But then an idea came to me.

"Wait," I said. "Let me see your phone." I snatched Brad's phone out of his hands and pulled up his Instagram. I played the video, which already had over a hundred views even though it hadn't been up longer than two minutes. I watched it twice. Neither time did the man seem to look at me or say anything. But I swore it had happened. He knew my name.

Brad and I made it to the park. Although it was quite chilly out, we grabbed a spot on a park bench.

We weren't sitting long before Sara Tompkins, Rachel Lewis, Josh Hartley, and Nelson Strong approached us. Sara walked right up to Brad and started talking. I was shocked. Not as shocked as Brad, though. I could feel his nervous energy radiating from his body. His hands were frozen in place on his phone, but his eyes were locked on Sara.

"Hi, Brad. How's it going? I mean, no. Wait. I'm Brad. How's Sara going? I mean … You're Brad, I'm Sara, how are you doing?" Brad completely fumbled his words. He was a mess. He couldn't even think straight, but Sara seemed to enjoy it. She was laughing.

"I believe you mean to say 'what's up?'" The two of them shared a laugh.

Rachel, Josh, and Nelson were all staring down at their cell phones in a small circle, laughing about something.

"That video was creepy!" Sara said. "Who was that guy?"

"Right?!" Brad responded. "Jessie and I were walking …"

Sara looked over at me and gave a small nod. She obviously wasn't interested in talking to me at all. Why would she? No one else did.

"And we saw that zombie guy! He legit looked like something straight out of a movie! It was kinda rad." Brad giggled as he spoke, very clearly proud of his social prowess.

"Yeah, and the guy knew my name …" I said, but Brad elbowed me in the ribs before I could finish.

"What was that, Jessie?" Sara responded.

"The guy—the weird zombie man—" But Brad cut me off again before I could finish.

"Yes, Jessie. The guy didn't even know his own name. Good call!"

Brad and Sara continued their awkward conversation for what seemed like forever. It mostly consisted of talking about different memes and videos from the last day or so. Everyone was using their phones—everyone except me. I just sat there on the park bench, staring off into the distance.

Brad and Sara had formed their own mini bubble of conversation with their phones out. Rachel, Josh and

Nelson continued on in their little circle, also looking down at their phones.

Brad was usually a good friend, but as soon as Sara walked up to him, he was completely hypnotized. I guess I don't blame him. Sara was one of the coolest girls in school.

"I can't believe how many likes you got!" Sara said.

"Right?! It totally took off," Brad bragged.

I knew Brad didn't mean to leave me out due to his undying love for Sara, but it made me feel even more alone. I just wished there were some way I could be a part of the group. I needed to find a way to get a cell phone. I knew right then that this could not continue. The entirety of my social life depended on it. Maybe I needed to ask for more allowance and save, or maybe I could try and pick up a shoveling job on the weekends. One thing was clear, though: I needed a phone, and I needed it ASAP.

On the walk back to our apartments, Brad's phone was blowing up even more than usual. It was buzz after buzz after buzz. We barely spoke because his phone kept going off with notifications about the video. People were commenting all kinds of wild things. He gained, like, a hundred followers from that one video.

"This guy's going to make me famous!" Brad spoke.

Maybe he would, I thought. This really was the end of my social life as we knew it. All because my parents won't buy me a phone.

I looked over at Brad, who was frowning. He looked

scared.

"What's wrong?" I said to him. He didn't respond. "Hello? Earth to Brad! Are you there? Do you copy?" Still nothing. I shook him, and he finally looked up.

"L-Look …" He stammered, his voice trembling.

Brad passed me his phone, but he wasn't trying to show me how many likes he had or that Sara was commenting. He was stunned because of a message that someone had left for him on the video. The message said:

"Hungry … So, so hungry … and now it's time to FEED!"

Chapter 4

I was shocked, just like Brad. The words crept into my brain and stuck there. They replayed in my mind over and over. It had to be fake, right? It had to be a scam.

"Dude, this is just one of those fake accounts. It's not real. Look at the name of the account," I said.

The name was just @Ghost. It freaked me out a little that there were no numbers or symbols. It wasn't common that someone's social media name was just one word. But that's also what made me realize it was a fake account.

"Don't even respond." I continued.

Brad was still quiet. He took a minute to answer me.

"I guess," he finally said. "But the whole thing is weirding me out now. Maybe I shouldn't have taken that video."

"It doesn't matter now—you already posted it, and you got to talk to Sara. Just let it go. These things happen every day on social media." I spoke as if I knew, but I really hadn't a clue. I was just trying to relax Brad. The whole situation was quite odd and eerie.

"I guess you're right," Brad answered.

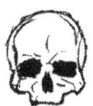

The walk back to our apartments was unusually quiet. We normally talked football and comics and joked about how we weren't going to do our math homework. But today, we were scared, nervous, and silent.

As we approached our apartments and got ready to say goodbye, Brad mentioned that he didn't want to talk about the zombie guy or the fact that he'd posted about it anymore. He promised to take the video down when he got home.

"Hey dude, I'm also sorry if I left you out of the convo back there. It's Sara! I go nuts when I'm around her!"

"I know, dude. It's cool. Buds for life." We fist bumped.

Most of me was relieved that Brad was going to take the video down. No one needed to see that anymore. But there was part of me that felt bad for Brad. Hopefully this didn't change his social status. I was totally off the social grid, but that didn't mean Brad also had to be.

I walked into my apartment and right up to my room. Buttons followed me in, curled up next to me, and at some point, I dozed off without even eating dinner.

The next morning, I shut my locker and found Brad waiting for me behind it. I jumped.

"Dude, don't scare me like that," I said.

"Jessie, seven hundred likes." Brad said.

"What?" I replied.

"My video has seven hundred likes!" Brad's eyes were lit up. "I'm going to be social media famous! Your best friend is going to be a star!"

At first, I wasn't sure what he was talking about. And then it hit me—Brad hadn't taken down the video.

"What video? Please don't tell me it's *the* video."

"The one with the zombie guy!" Brad was glowing.

I had never seen him like this before. Sure, I'd seen him happy, but he was completely transfixed.

"I really was going to take it down, but it just kept blowing up! I kept getting more and more likes. How can I take it down? This could be my ticket!" Brad said. "I kept getting notifications throughout the night."

"Let me see," I said, grabbing at Brad's phone.

He showed me his Instagram. The video was now up to 710 likes.

"I guess that's cool," I said, not really knowing how to respond. I didn't want to watch the video again, but Brad kind of forced me to.

"This is the best part," he said as the man's raggedy skull turned to face the camera.

It was like watching it for the first time. Something just wasn't right about the man, the video, the whole thing. Every time I watched it or thought about it, my stomach curled up into a ball. An emptiness seeped in.

"Hey, Brad," a voice said.

At first, I didn't recognize the voice. I surveyed the area and saw Mallory Stevens walking with Julie Birch. Both were waving at Brad.

This was unbelievable. Brad's entire social status was blowing up. The more likes he got, the more popular he was. Mallory Stevens and Julie Birch were WAY too popular to be saying hi to Brad. This left me feeling lonely again.

"Dude, did you see that?" Brad asked.

"Yes, I saw it," I replied.

"That was Mallory Stevens. She's, like, the hottest girl in eighth grade." Brad said.

"Yeah, duh, brainiac. I know that," I said as I bumped Brad's shoulder and walked past him.

There was so much going through my mind. Although not much had happened, it felt like so much was changing. Brad was becoming the hit of our eighth-grade class in the blink of an eye. And it was all because of that stupid video he'd uploaded. Why couldn't I have taken that video? Why couldn't Mallory Stevens be saying hi to me? And then I lost myself in a daydream where I was walking alongside Mallory on our way to science class.

"Jess. Hey, Jess Man." I felt something hit my shoulder. It was Brad punching me.

"Ouch, dude, what the—?" I rubbed my shoulder. "That hurt!"

"Sorry, dude, but you weren't responding. You were zombified," Brad replied.

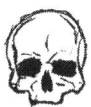

Brad and I made our way to science class with the worst teacher on planet Earth, Mr. Miller. Everyone in the school hated him so much, as he was an even more vile creature than was indicated by his nickname, Miller the Killer. He barely taught anything. If you spoke in class or weren't prepared, he would scream in your face.

Quite frankly, it was a shock that he still had a job. But he was besties with Principal Johnson, so Miller being fired was out of the question. The two of them were like two peas in a pod.

Miller the Killer had been teaching for more than thirty years and just didn't like kids. He hated Brad and me most of all, probably because we are often unprepared. We did fine in school, but we were usually the type to catch up rather than do the work every day. We sat down and braced ourselves for forty-four minutes of hell.

"Okay, class." We were silent as he spoke. "Today we are going to be taking a look at mass and weight. Therefore, we need to understand volume and density," the Killer went on.

I looked over at Brad, who was already half asleep. And then I noticed that Josh Hartley was doing something in his bag on the floor. Was he looking at his phone?

I tried to get a closer look, but then Miller walked down my row of seats. I instantly propped myself back up, pretending to listen.

Josh looking at his phone would be a seriously risky move. Miller the Killer had been known to take phones on sight and keep them until people's parents came to school to pick them up.

When Mr. Miller was on the complete opposite side of the room, I tried to get Josh's attention. "Pssst." I wanted to warn him that he would get caught and that Miller was the worst when he got your phone. "Josh …" I tried to whisper, but it came out louder than I expected.

"Mr. Davidson!" The Killer was angry. He screamed at me. "How DARE you interrupt me while I'm speaking? I hope you have a perfectly reasonable explanation for this. In fact, you MUST … because you will be telling it to me during lunch detention. And it better be good."

"But Mr. Miller …"

Before I could even finish my thought, he went on about the formula for figuring out an object's mass.

Well, isn't this great, I thought. Not only was I the only kid in eighth grade without a phone, but I'd also pulled lunch detention for trying to warn Josh Hartley to put away *his* phone.

Don't overreact, Jessie, I thought. *You were just trying to be a good friend, that's all. You'll serve your lunch detention and move on.*

Everywhere I turned, cell phones were consuming me. Either I was wishing I had one or hearing about Brad's social media, and now I'd gotten in trouble for trying to warn Josh.

I had never wanted anything in my life more than I wanted a cell phone in that moment. However, I was about to find out that not having a phone was way worse than I'd ever imagined.

"Okay, class, here is what I would like to do." Mr. Miller was handing out a worksheet as he spoke. When thinking about mass and density, we need to think about the size and weight of the object…"

"Psst." A whisper called out to me. "Hey Jessie…" I looked over to the desk next to me. It was Nelson Strong calling to me.

Keeping my voice as low as possible, I looked over at him glowingly and responded, "What's up, Strong?"

"Dude, check this out," he whispered back, handing me his phone.

Feeling the weight of his phone in my hand was nice. I quickly tucked it in the fold of my hoodie and looked down to see what it was, but before I even had a chance to see, Miller went off.

"Is that what I think it is?" Miller the Killer shouted, and I instantly jumped, pocketing the phone into my jeans.

"Um, no, Mr. Miller. What are you referring to?"

"Oh, dear Mr. Jessie Davidson. I'm referring to the small black box inside your pocket. I believe we refer to them as cell phones."

"Uh, yeah Mr. Miller. I'm aware of what a cell phone is…" But before I could even finish my thought, Miller the Killer exploded into a rage.

"ARE YOU TELLING ME I'M A LIAR, DAVIDSON?" Mr. Miller ducked down low to meet my eyes directly. Both of his hands held down my desk and were rattling it, vibrating the wood. The glisten from his bald head shone on my face. There were beads of sweat running down it. "Are you MOCKING me, Mr. Davidson?"

I already had lunch detention with Miller, so I had no choice but to cover myself and lie. If he caught me with Nelson's phone, I would be dead meat. He would call my parents to come into school for a conference. "Mr. Miller, I promise you I'm not doing anything wrong. I don't even have a cell phone…"

"Well alright, Mr. Davidson. That's good, yes." Mr. Miller spoke calmly now. He lifted his hands off of my desk and stood up straight and tall. "I believe you. Right class? We believe him?" Mr. Miller scanned the silent group of students sitting at their desks in front of him. Everyone had their hands folded together in a neat pile on top of their desk. Not a sound could be heard. "Now please, Mr. Davidson, be a good lad, do me a favor and stand up."

I gently put my hands to the back pocket of my jeans to remind myself that Nelson's phone was in there. It was, so I stood up.

"Now empty the pocket of your hooded sweatshirt, Mr. Davidson."

I obliged with his request, and to his chagrin, there was nothing there.

I knew I would regret it, but trying to cover for myself, I figured I would just tell the truth. "Mr. Miller, If you thought you saw a cell phone, you are wrong. I don't even own one. My parents refuse to get me one. They don't think I'm old enough." There were small fits of giggles coming from pockets around the room as I said it, but I kept my eyes straight ahead at Miller.

"Ah, I see. It seems you've tricked me, Mr. Davidson. Well I'll tell you this, and don't you forget it, lad." Miller now stood over me. His hulking frame dwarfed me. "I will be watching your every move. If I find out that you lied to me, son, it will be the biggest mistake of your life." And with those words, Miller stood tall and went back to the mass and weight.

I looked over to my left, mostly because Miller's spit and sweat had projectile splashed onto my face, and saw Julie Birch with her phone out videotaping the whole thing.

Oh no, this is not good, I thought. *This is so embarrassing.* And the worst part was that Miller's back was to her, so he couldn't see a thing. I knew this would be uploaded to social media within moments for the whole world to see. And even worse than that was the amount of followers Julie had.

Chapter 5

Lunchtime. Finally, lunchtime.

On any normal day, this would have been the best period. I would have been eating my pizza bites and drinking my chocolate milk. Brad and I probably would've been having a thumb war, arguing about how my thumb covered his for a full three seconds before he lifted it up. But not today's lunch. Today's lunch was going to be the worst period *ever*.

I entered Miller's room at the start of fifth period. "Did I give you permission to enter the room, Mr. Davidson?"

"No, Mr. Miller, I—" *This is going to be just great*, I thought.

"Please exit the room and reenter. But first, please knock. It's impolite to do otherwise." He stared me directly in the eye and watched me leave. He closed the door behind me and went back to his desk while I stood out in the hallway.

I can't believe this guy, I thought. I knocked on the door and Miller stood up from his chair not a moment after sitting down and came over to open it. "Mr. Davidson, you are late. Next time, that will cost you another day's lunch detention."

I walked into the room and took a seat at my usual desk. The room was so empty without other students. Miller closed the door behind me.

"You know, Mr. Davidson, we live in quite a peculiar day and age. When I was young like you, we didn't have cell phones. Heck, we barely even had television. I used to sharpen my mind with a good book every day. Kids today have no idea what it means to use their brains. All they care about is the next instant video or mean."

"I think you mean meme, Mr. Miller," I responded.

"That's what I said, young man. Do not patronize me," Miller said.

"Yes, Mr. Miller."

I continued. "Mr. Miller. I want to apologize for earlier today. I know you think you saw a cell phone in my hand, but it wasn't. I don't even own one." There's no way Miller was going to believe me, but I figured at this point it couldn't hurt to try.

"Ah, yes," Miller spoke. "Well, don't take me for a fool, Mr. Davidson. Believe me, it will be the last thing you do. I know what I saw."

Miller pulled up a chair, sat down next to me, sighed and began again. "Okay, Mr. Davidson, I'll play your game. Why is it that you don't have a phone then? Are you not like your friends, the rest of these delinquents?"

"Well, I do want one, Mr. Miller. But my parents don't feel I should have one just yet. They keep saying I need to be a little older." This thought angered me. Maybe they would finally see that I needed one after this incident. The truth was, Dad was usually set in his ways. They would stick to their guns and find another plausible solution before giving in and getting me a phone, I was sure of it.

"Well, good on them! Maybe you do have a small bone of integrity after all, Mr. Davidson," Miller said.

"Yeah. Thanks, Mr. Miller."

"Don't let this fool you, though, Mr. Davidson. You are insubordinate, and because of that, you are here. Now, don't talk and don't move. Your lunch detention officially begins"—Miller looked at his watch—"now."

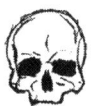

That was hell, I thought as I exited Miller's room. Brad was waiting for me right outside his door.

"That bad, huh?" he said.

"Think about your worst nightmare. This was way worse than that could ever be," I replied.

We laughed and walked to sixth period. On our

walk, I couldn't help but notice people staring at me.

Marcus Sneadleman walked right by us, and at first, it seemed like he was just laughing. But then I noticed he was looking directly at me, then down at his phone, then back up at me. *I get it, I don't have a phone*, I wanted to say. This shouldn't have been news to anyone.

Then it was Joseph Levine and Tom Schneider, followed by Sara and Rachel. Eventually, I realized that everyone was watching some video, then laughing at me as I walked by them. My stomach dropped, because deep down inside, I knew what was happening. There could only be one explanation.

"Hey, dude, remember that time Miller screamed at you in science class and totally embarrassed you?" Brad said.

"You mean this morning?" I responded.

"Was that this morning?" Brad spoke sarcastically as he put his arm around me. "Yeah, well, the thing is …"

I already knew what he was about to say. The rest of his words were just jumbled noise. Julie Birch had posted the video of Miller and me from this morning. But it was so much worse than that. Julie had face swapped a cell phone onto my head with a speech bubble that said: *"Mommy and daddy won't get a phone for their wittle baby!"* It was so childish and dumb, but they made me look ridiculous. I was the laughingstock of the eighth grade.

Brad showed me the video on our walk home from school. It had over five hundred views, and people were commenting left and right. Even worse, there were ninth graders commenting also.

"Don't be such a delinquent, Davidson!" one kid wrote.

"Welcome to 2019, loser!" another kid wrote.

"It's not that bad," Brad said. "Who cares what those people think?"

"Those people?" I said. "*Those* people? Those people are the entire eighth grade! I'm done. This is it. My entire life, this is going to follow me. I'm forever going to be the kid who doesn't have a phone. People will always remember this, Brad."

"Look, just try not to think about it, all right? I've got your back. Don't worry about those comments. They don't know what they're talking about." Brad tried to calm me down. It helped, I guess. "Buds for life, dude."

"Yeah, buds for life." I fist-bumped Brad, and he went on to his apartment. I appreciated him as a friend, I really did. But this was something he couldn't help with. I wished that wasn't the case, but I just needed to start accepting the fact that this was my reality now and that wasn't going to change anytime soon.

I walked into my house. "Mom?" No response.

"Dad?" Nothing. It seemed like no one was home.

Buttons came waddling up to me, his tail wagging. "There's my buddy." I bent down and lifted him up into a hug. "At least I have you, Butts." He licked my face. I fed him his normal afternoon snack, and he was a happy puppy.

I wanted to curl up in a ball and cry. Brad was home, probably talking to Sara on social media, my parents were out, and I felt so alone again. A feeling I was becoming way too familiar with. At least I had Buttons.

Maybe phones were so powerful because they helped kids get through difficult times, like now. They helped kids not feel alone when they otherwise would have. Regardless, I wouldn't know, because I'd never felt more distant from the world than I did at that moment.

I tried to read a book, but I didn't get through more than a page or two before getting bored. Then I tried taking a nap, but every time I shut my eyes, my mind kept zipping right back to Miller and the video of me in class. I felt like I was locked up in a prison. There was no one around me, nothing to do. The only thing missing were the bars on my windows.

"Brad, do you copy?" I tried to reach him on our walkies. No response.

"I repeat, Jessie to Brad, do you copy?" Nothing.

I lay there for the next fifteen minutes trying to reach him. I stopped pressing the button after a while. I knew he wasn't there; I just wanted to talk to someone. The silence was deafening.

"Come on, Butts." I put the walkie down and made my way into the office. My parents kept a desktop computer that they allowed me to use strictly for my email. They had all kinds of parental regulations preventing me from doing anything of note on the internet.

I logged into my email, JDKIDBUTTS@gmail.com. My address was the same one I had been using since I was eight. It was childish, but most of my email was spam, anyway. I'd made it when we'd first gotten Buttons, and I was still a kid, so I'd kept it. Seventy-five unopened emails. That was quite a bit.

I began scrolling through the long list. One by one, I went through them and deleted. It was boring, but at least It was keeping me busy. I stopped, though, when I reached the very last email. It had no subject, but the sender's address was one I had seen before, one that had me terrified. The address was one word: @GHOST.

I remembered instantly where I had seen that address before. It wasn't in an email but on Brad's Instagram post. It had said, *"Hungry … So, so hungry … and now it's time to FEED!"*

When I opened it up, the message was blank. I looked for any type of text, but there was nothing.

After a few moments of staring at the bizarre email, I heard something. A scratching or screeching noise. It sounded like someone was playing the most out-of-tune, rusty violin on earth. I looked around the room, but there was no one there. The noise got louder. I realized it was coming from the computer. It got even louder, and then a voice spoke. The voice was terrifying. It was as if that rusty violin were able to speak, and it spoke deeply and slowly.

"So hungry. I need to eaaat. I need to feed nowww!"

Chapter 6

I ran back into my bedroom to call Brad on the walkie-talkie, Buttons trailing behind me. "BRAD! BRAD! ANSWER ME, PLEASE!"

After a moment or two, Brad's groggy voice replied, "Yeah, yeah. I'm up. What's going on?"

"Get over here now," I said, my mind racing.

The intercom buzzed a few minutes later, and it scared me. Waiting by the button, I let Brad in immediately. He was in his pajamas, and his brown hair was a complete mess. "You're not gonna believe this." I was breathing heavily as I spoke.

I led Brad upstairs and into the office. "Check this out," I said.

I went back into my emails, but I couldn't find the one from @Ghost.

"Where are you?! You were just right here!" Had I

accidentally deleted it? *I couldn't have,* I thought. I supposed I had jumped in fright when I'd heard that voice call out to me. Maybe my finger had moved accidentally and deleted it? That was a possibility.

"What, man? What's going on? Did Miller email you?" Brad said.

"No, no, no, this can't be happening." I was frantic, trying to figure out what had happened. I opened emails, crazily looking in my previously read messages and in the trash.

"Okay, Brad. You know me, right? You trust me?" I suddenly realized how foolish I looked. I had called Brad over for what seemed like an emergency but in actuality seemed to be nothing.

"Of course, man. What happened? Just tell me." Brad seemed genuinely concerned.

I tried to think of the best way to tell him about the email and the voice without sounding crazy. I mean, what was I supposed to say? *I think a ghost just emailed me?* I realized how ridiculous that sounded.

"Okay, do you remember that @Ghost account that commented on your Instagram post?" I said.

"Yeah, the scammer. I remember. Continue."

"Okay, well. I got an email from the same account. But this time, there was a voice message that went along with it. It said it was so hungry and that it needed to feed."

What was I saying? This must have sounded crazy to Brad. There was no way he was going to buy this.

Brad looked confused. "Okay, just to be clear, you brought me here to tell me about your spam emails?"

"No, this wasn't spam! This was something else! I swear it. I wish you could have heard the voice. It was terrifying," I said.

"Dude, I get that it might seem real and scary. Most of these spam accounts do. I get these all the time on social media. There are crazy people out there, man. There are *millions* of these fake accounts sending out scary stuff all the time just to mess with people! It's one of the downsides of the internet. I just think it's funny. You don't have a phone, so you're probably not used to it, but this seriously happens all the time."

Brad was quite convincing. *Why hadn't I thought of that?* Of course it was just a spam account. There was no way an actual ghost had emailed me.

Brad helped calm me down. Everything he said made sense to me. I began to think I had overreacted a tad, but the voice had seemed so real, so scary. So dead. And I couldn't shake the feeling that had come over me when the voice message had played—a coldness that sent shivers down to my bones. I hadn't realized it until now, but I was freezing.

"Everything's going to be fine, dude. Promise." Brad was right. This was such a common thing. I was just not used to it. All the more reason I needed a phone.

Trying not to think about the email, I shifted the conversation back to wanting a cell phone. "How can I raise money?" I asked Brad as I plopped down onto my bed.

"This again?" Brad replied.

"Yes, this again. I can't go on like this. I feel like a caveman. I can't be a normally functioning eighth grade kid without a phone. Look at the facts: I just called you because I thought a ghost was emailing me. I think I'm losing it, dude. That's not normal."

Brad sat and thought for a moment before responding. "I suppose we could have a bake sale?"

Brad's idea wasn't bad, but I doubted we would make anywhere near enough money for me to get a phone. New phones cost, like, five hundred dollars plus.

"Maybe you can ask Geno if you can help out at the cart?"

Also not a bad idea, but I highly doubted Geno made enough money to pay me anything. I bet he barely made enough money to stay afloat himself. Plus, he already helped us out all the time with free sandwiches.

"I suppose you could steal one?" Brad was being serious. I looked at him, then threw a pillow at him.

"I'm not stealing anything, dingus!" I yelled at him.

"All right, well, at least I'm trying, here! I don't see you making any suggestions."

Brad was right. His suggestions were better than nothing.

And then it hit me. "Wait a minute. Why don't we sell a bunch of things? I have so much old stuff just lying around. What if I sell it? Most of it is used, but if I sold enough things, I might be able to scrounge up just enough to get a used phone."

I looked around my room. I had an old PlayStation that was probably worth fifty bucks at most. I had an old iPod that I could sell. My old soccer ball, a tennis racket, a pair of basketball shoes. All of these things combined might actually work give me a fighting chance.

Brad agreed, and so we had a plan. I was going to sell my things.

Over the next week, I began selling off my old stuff. Brad took pictures with his phone and posted them on social media so that anyone who was interested could contact him. Some stuff sold quickly, like my old basketball shoes. I got a solid forty bucks for those.

Friday morning, Brad and I walked to school together, as usual. For the first time in a long while, I felt good. I was starting to feel hopeful. I also felt like I was being a responsible young adult. This was how it was done: the American dream. If you wanted something, you couldn't wait for it to come to you. You had to go out there and get it yourself. That was exactly what I was doing, and there was nothing that could stop me now. Or so I thought.

"Ey, Geno!" Brad said.

"Boys, boys! What can I do for you today?" Geno responded.

"The usual, Geno, and keep the change," I replied with a big smile on my face.

I paid Geno with a five-dollar bill. I knew I needed to cut corners and save every chance I got if I was going to get my phone, but I also believed in good karma. And Geno was always hooking us up, so I felt good about paying him.

"My man! I always knew I liked you boys." Geno fist-bumped us both as we turned to go.

"Dude, Geno hooked it up! Do you see the amount of bacon on this thing?" Brad's sandwich was overflowing with crispy, delicious bacon. Some of Geno's finest work.

The school day flew by relatively quickly. Even Miller's class seemed all right. I was so excited to be closer to my cell phone goal that everything else seemed small. In just a few more days, everything would be fixed. I would finally be able to afford my cell phone, and then I would be all over social media. I needed to start thinking about my Instagram handle. So exciting!

The weekend was finally here. Brad and I left school

and started walking our normal route.

"Dude, let's go to the park. Sara, Rachel, Josh, and Nelson are all going to hang out!" Brad was looking down at the text Sara had just sent him.

I paused to think about how to respond. I had gotten so fed up with Sara and her friends over the past few weeks, and I knew how this would go. We would arrive, they would say hi, and then everyone would converse only about what was on their cell phones. I would be left out, as usual.

"Sure, let's go," I said, surprising myself.

"That's the spirit—there's my dawg!" Brad was shocked, too.

I just had a new confidence in me since I'd started raising money. I felt comfortable with myself. I was going to get my cell phone, and I wanted them to know about it.

We walked down 86th street and made our way to the park entrance. The park seemed relatively quiet for a Friday afternoon.

It wasn't long after we entered the park that a cold shiver ran down my spine. It was the same feeling I'd felt when Ghost had sent me that email. Like there was someone watching me. I did a full 360 and looked around the park. There was no one around.

"You all right, Jess?" Brad asked me.

"Yeah, fine," I lied.

I wiped my forehead with my arm and realized I was sweating. I felt cold, feverish. *What was happening,* I thought?

We kept walking, and I got dizzier. "Dude, you don't look so hot. You're super pale, and you're sweating," Brad said.

"No, I'm fine. I'm … fine." I was not fine.

What happened next ruined everything. All my hard work, all my bright ideas. Gone. Poof. Donezo.

I was barely able to make out the figure that came out of the trees, but I definitely saw someone. They were draped in a black hood and a long robe that looked like a black sheet. I heard Brad say something, but my hearing was muted, my vision was spotty, and my head throbbed. Before I realized that I was being robbed, I fainted.

"Jessie … Jessie, wake up." My eyelids fluttered open and pain shot through my head.

"Dude, that was insane, are you okay?" Brad said.

I slowly sat up. "Wh-what happened?" I asked.

"Do you want me to tell the truth or lie?"

I had to think for a minute. Everything was going so well, I wasn't sure I wanted to hear any bad truths. "Truth," I said.

"Some madman just ran out of the trees and stole your bag. Along with all the money you've raised." Brad pulled back an uneven smile, as if to say he was sorry.

It took me a minute to process what Brad had said and another to realize that my life was ruined, again. *Why is this happening to me?*

"Just be cool," Brad said. "Everything's going to be okay."

I stood up and flipped out. "NO! Everything's NOT going to be okay, Brad!" I was shouting now. "I'm never going to be popular, I'm NEVER going to be a normal kid, and I'm NEVER GOING TO HAVE A CELL PHONE!"

Even louder than I was shouting before, I yelled, "I WISH I WERE DEAD!"

Chapter 7

I'd never felt more discouraged in my life. All my hard work, gone in a flash.

The next week at school was a real drag. I tried to pay attention and move on with my life, but my mind was simply turned off. I was mentally checked out. Even worse, I had to see Cory Mann in my old basketball shoes every day. Brad also told me Josh and Nelson posted pictures of themselves playing my old PlayStation every day.

I wasn't mad at them for enjoying the things I'd sold them. I was just upset. Nothing ever seemed to break right for me.

Brad came by Tuesday night, but for the most part, he spent the week flirting with Sara or meeting up with her at the park to talk about the latest social media crazes. Oh yeah, and Josh's big party was coming up, and I, of course, wasn't invited.

"Knock, knock!" Mom and Dad checked in before entering my room.

"It's open," I said.

"Hey there, squirt. You all right? Mom and I are a little worried about ya."

"Then how about you get me a cell phone? That would solve all of my issues," I said, frustrated.

Mom and Dad looked at each other and then at me. I knew I was being difficult and that it wouldn't get me anywhere, but I didn't care anymore. What was the harm in giving some attitude? My parents deserved at least some of the shade I was throwing at them.

"Look, we get it. Mom and I get it. I know it's hard to understand, but we were both kids once, too. And we both know what it feels like to be left out. The point is that we want you to get through this, and we have your back. This is a good test for you. Prove to yourself that you don't need a cell phone to fit in. We know how great you are. No cell phone can change that," Dad said.

"Sure, Dad." Again, they looked at each other and sighed. I was being extremely sarcastic, and they knew it. I just wanted to be left alone. Alone with my thoughts and my dog. I wanted to lie there and live out the rest of my days as a big loser.

My parents were upset for me—I knew that. I could tell by my dad's expression. I could see it in his eyes. But they took the hint that I wanted to be alone. They left my room, and Buttons nuzzled into my side.

"You okay, Butts?" He looked at me with his bulbous brown eyes. "Need to go to the bathroom?" As soon as I got up from bed, he jumped off and followed me, tongue lolling out of his mouth.

"I'm taking Butts out for a walk," I said to my parents as I put his leash on.

We stepped out into the brisk night and were on our way. We started along our normal route, Buttons smelling and licking all his favorite spots. After he went to the bathroom, I didn't feel like going back just yet. The quietness of the walk was peaceful, so we kept on, Buttons by my side. Again, his tongue was sticking out. He approved of the longer walk.

We made our way off our normal route and ended up at the entrance to the park. "Do you want to go to the park, Butts? Yeah, boy? Go to the park?" I said to him excitedly.

He just kind of stood there, but if there was one thing I knew about Buttons, it was that he loved to walk. Anytime, anyplace.

Even though it was against my parents' rules, I went into the park. Dad always said to *make sure you're around people, squirt!* The park was a big no-no once it got dark. *What do they know?* I thought. *When has listening to them ever gotten me anywhere?*

I had been so angry lately. I felt like my mind was racing a million miles a minute. A thirteen-year-old kid should not be this stressed! So much was working against me. But in that moment, as I walked Buttons through Central Park, I felt calm. I felt good. For just one moment, my troubles were gone. I could breathe. I wasn't thinking about Miller, or social media, or Brad and Sara. Most of all, I wasn't thinking about the fact that I would never, ever own a cell phone.

That feeling only lasted a short time, though. I was suddenly cold, just like the feeling I'd had when Ghost had emailed me. The hairs on the back of my neck stood up. I brushed them with my hand. Buttons barked.

"What is it, Butts? Everything okay?" I bent down to his level.

He was barking and looking at something. I tried to make out what was upsetting him, but I couldn't figure it out.

He pulled the leash a few steps farther along the path, and then I saw what he was barking at. Just beyond some trees that separated the path from the woods, there was a small light. It was dim, but it was most definitely there. I walked a few more steps before Buttons started growling. My eyes stayed focused on the light.

Buttons and I walked slowly through the trees, and the light shone bigger, brighter. As we got nearer, I discovered it was coming from a lantern.

We pushed through the remaining trees and walked out into a clearing. There was a colorful, rustic-looking carpet spread out on the grass. A lantern lit up each corner.

I was confused by what I was seeing. Buttons's barks turned to low hisses and growls. He seemed to be shaking. Even though he wouldn't hurt a fly, he bared his teeth. There was something here he didn't like.

"Looking for something in particular, my boy?" said a voice.

I turned around quickly. Buttons was going nuts.

"Uh, hi. No, thank you, sir. My dog and I were just passing through, and I think we'll be on our way now." I started to turn around when the man spoke again.

"Leaving so soon?" he said. "Why don't you take a look around, stay for a minute? I have something that might interest you." The man was draped in black cloth, and a hood covered his face except for his eyes. I could see through his hood the darkest, greenest eyes.

"YOU!" I exclaimed, realizing who I had come face-to-face with. "I know you! You're the guy who robbed me!"

I was immediately filled with rage. This was the guy who'd ruined my life. "You destroyed everything, you jerk! Why did you do that?"

"Oh, yes. I do apologize for that, but I think it will all be for the best, my boy. You see, it's no coincidence that brought us together tonight. I've been watching you. And I think you are perfect." The man spoke with a purpose.

What was this guy talking about? I wasn't perfect at anything.

"Yeah, whatever, man. Are you going to give me back my money or not? I'm not in the mood to argue. My whole social life is officially over, thanks to you. So, if you don't mind, I'll be on my way. Back to my little, boring life without a cell phone."

I stared into the dark abyss of the man's hood, waiting for a reply. There was nothing. Then he finally said, "Perhaps we can make a trade. I've caused you so much harm and grief, and I do feel terrible about it."

The hooded man began circling the carpet, getting closer to me. "Allow me to make it up to you. As I said, I've been watching you, and I think you are perfect. You are just the one!" Slowly, he took off his hood and revealed the horrible skin underneath. It was all raggedy and thin. The man was speaking without lips, just greenish skin that layered in thin folds down to his mouth. He had no teeth, and there were green and purple scars everywhere. This was the same man Brad and I saw running rampant and scaring people a few weeks ago.

My mind went racing back to that moment on the street. "You. How did you know my name?" The words came out of my mouth slowly. My eyes were locked on this man's face. How was he even alive? He was grotesque. No wonder he covered his whole body up.

"I know quite a bit about you, Jessie Davidson. Like I said, I've been watching you. You are a very special boy." The man was only a few feet away from me now.

I thought about my next move carefully. I thought

about just running and ditching this whole situation. Butts and I could run home together and curl up in my cozy bed. There was something keeping me there, though. My body tensed and I couldn't gather the courage to move. After a moment's hesitation, one leg began to work, and then the other.

"Yeah, whatever. I'm outta here, old man. Have a nice life. Whatever's left of it." I started to walk away, but the man jumped in front of me.

"Are you excited for Josh's party?" he asked.

How did he know about Josh's party?

"I ... I wasn't invited to Josh's party," I stammered.

"Pity," the man said. "What if I could help with that?" Every syllable he spoke came out as a dark and hissy whisper.

This guy was bonkers, but I couldn't help but listen to him.

The man's thin and withered eyebrows shot up as he prepared to speak again. He tried to get words out but instead turned his head and let out a putrid fit of coughing. As it subsided, the man slowly, carefully turned back around to face me.

"I think I have something that might interest you, dear boy," the man said, and pulled what looked like a cell phone out of his robe pocket. It was jet black, and it looked brand new. The shiny glass reflected the light of the lanterns.

The man pressed the on button and the phone lit up right before my eyes. The background was a picture of me lying down with Buttons in my room, smiling widely. How was this possible? As scared and creeped out as I was, I was glued to the phone in his hand. My gaze was the sun beating down on a late-summer afternoon. I wanted so badly to have the phone. This was too good to be true.

Not taking my eyes off the phone, I managed to get out the words, "What's in it for you?" I hesitated before speaking again. "You already took all my money. I have nothing left to give you."

"Give me?" The man seemed confused. "I do not wish for you to *give* me anything, boy. All I ask is for one simple thing in return: a promise. And if you agree to this promise, the phone is yours. To keep. Forever." His throaty voice was deeper now.

"A promise," I said. "All you want me to do is promise you something?"

"That is correct, boy."

"All right, old man. Out with it. What is this promise?" I knew I should have left already, but the phone had grabbed my attention and wouldn't let go. I was caught in its beam of light. It was attracting me more with each passing second.

Who just gave away a phone like this? Maybe the man felt bad for mugging me. Who cared? This was my opportunity!

"Promise that you'll accept this gift from me, this cell phone. It's yours forever. But you may *never* return it. You must keep it, and you may never give it back to me." The man's harsh voice managed to get out the words, but he sounded like he was in pain.

I was shocked. All I had to do to get this brand-new phone was promise that I would never give it back to him?

"Are you messing with me? Is this some kind of reality show? Is there someone in the woods filming this for Instagram?" I looked all around me, past the colorful carpet and off into the trees. I turned around to see if there was anything behind me.

"I assure you this is no trick, boy. Agree to my deal, and the phone is yours. I beg you. Promise me, and all of your hopes and desires will come true." There was desperation in his voice.

The man placed the phone in my hand. I felt the smooth glass. The weight of it on my palm felt sensational.

"We have a deal." And I squeezed the phone hard and ran back toward my apartment, Buttons following close behind.

When I reached a clearing near the entrance of the park, I thought I heard a laugh echoing from deep within the woods. I told myself it was probably Buttons slobbering on something. But as I would find out soon enough, I was sadly mistaken.

Chapter 8

I made it home quickly and opened the door. I slammed it shut and leaned against it. Buttons was staring up at me with wide eyes.

Mom and Dad were sitting in the kitchen. Dad was reading the paper and Mom was sipping a cup of tea, also reading.

"Hey Mom, hey Dad." I was out of breath.

And before they even responded, I dashed upstairs to my room. I closed the door behind me and locked it.

I pulled the phone out of my pocket and placed it on the bed. I was still in shock. I had a phone. It was here with me, in my possession.

My mind was racing: the man in the park, the carpet, the whole thing. Did all of it really happen? Surely it had been a dream. But there on my bed, staring back at me, was a cell phone. I had what I wanted, and I never had to see or deal with that crazy man ever again.

My next thought was that I had to tell Brad. I went to grab my walkie, but then realized I had a phone. I knew Brad's number by heart, so I went into my contacts to type it in, but I found something very odd. There was a long list of contacts already stored in my phone.

I looked through them, and there was "Brad Best Friend." I clicked on his name and there it was: Brad's number. It was already saved. *This just keeps getting better and better.* The list of contacts was quite long, and as I read through them—Sara, Josh, Nelson, Marcus Sneadleman—I realized every number I needed was already stored in my phone. It had been programmed in advance. Surely that wasn't how phones worked, though. Normally you needed to upload your contacts yourself, right?

Maybe this is a super *smartphone*, I thought. I clicked on Brad's number to call him.

I tried calling twice, but he didn't answer. He probably ignored unknown numbers, so I texted him.

Brad, don't ask questions, just get over here. NOW! Jessie

Within moments, he responded:

Dude, you got a phone?!?! LOL … on my way!

A few minutes later, Brad was at my front door. As

soon as I opened it, he called out, "Dude, I can't believe your parents got you—"

I covered his mouth with my hand and steered him toward the staircase.

"MMmF, mmfff." I felt Brad's moist tongue wetting my palm as he tried to speak. It was worse than getting licked by Buttons.

My parents responded, "Oh, hi, Bradley. What was that? What did we get—"

"Oh, nothing, Mom. Brad and I are going up to my room, thanks! Love you!" I rushed Brad up to my room and slammed the door shut, locking it behind me.

"You. Are. Not. Going. To Believe this." My eyes lit up as I spoke. I pulled the phone out of my pocket and placed it in Brad's hand.

"I must say," Brad said slowly, "I never thought this day would come, Jessie Davidson. Welcome to the world. It's a pleasure to have you on board."

Still in shock, I was glowing. My smile stretched from ear to ear. "I'm just as excited as you are, dude. But you *cannot* say anything to my parents. They don't know about it."

"How do they not know about it? Who got you the phone?" Brad said.

Although I never lied to Brad, I debated doing so now. Friends didn't lie, but I didn't know if he would believe the truth. I wasn't even sure *I* believed the truth. "Do you the want the real story or the fake story?" I said.

"Um, the real story?" Brad sounded slightly confused.

Here goes, I thought. "Okay, remember the guy with the long, dark, hooded robe ... the one you took the video of?" I walked him through the whole ordeal, beginning to end: my walk with Butts in the park, the weirdly vibrant carpet, and then eventually, the man and his promise.

"So, just to be clear ... the dude just gave it to you? No money, nothing? 'Here you go, here's this brand-new phone?'" Brad couldn't believe what he was hearing.

"That is correct," I said.

"My first thought is, O. M. G. That is the best thing ever. Holy moly. My second thought is, this is super weird, and I'm kind of worried."

"I know it seems odd." I realized Brad probably thought I was losing it, but it had all been real. This had all really happened.

Now that I had a cell phone, it was like the weight of the world had been lifted from my shoulders. Why was it so weird that something good had finally happened to me? So much had gone wrong. I just felt good for a change.

The excitement of having the phone was slightly too much for me to handle. I couldn't contain myself; I didn't know how to react. "I deserve a cell phone," I snapped at Brad. "Why should everyone else have one and not me?"

"Yeah, I get all that, dude. But don't you think you should tell your parents?" Brad responded. "Can we at least agree that it seems just a tad weird that this man showed up in the middle of the park to give you a cell phone?"

"Why can't you just be happy for me?!" I said angrily. "Finally, *one* good thing happens to me, and you can't accept that?"

Brad and I glared at each other. We looked directly into each other's eyes, staring each other down.

Suddenly, I wasn't sure what had come over me or why I'd shouted at Brad like that. I quickly apologized.

"It's all right, dude. I'm happy for you, I really am. The whole thing just creeps me out, I guess." Brad held the phone in his hands, admiring it's new, sleek shine.

"You're right. I'm sorry for snapping. I guess I'm just so excited. I can't wait to get on social media!" I grabbed my phone from Brad's hand and plopped down on my bed.

I thought about Brad's concerns for a moment. A large part of me knew he was right. This whole thing was too weird. But another large part of me didn't care. There was a voice inside of me saying, *This is everything you've ever wanted. Don't let anyone or anything ruin this.*

"Also, Jess Man, one more thing," Brad said. "When you called, the number that came up was odd. It was all ones. It came up as 111-111-1111."

I stayed up late that night. Aside from the fact that I was too excited to sleep, I was busy setting my phone up. I did find some more weird little quirks about it that didn't seem too normal. The first was the internet connection. When I went into my settings, there was no option for Wi-Fi.

That wasn't the weirdest part, though. The weirdest part was that the internet worked, and it worked well. It was extremely fast and smooth. Not only that, but my browser history was already stocked with all my favorite websites, like ESPN.

I went ahead and downloaded all the apps I wanted for sports and social media. Now I just needed to set up my profiles. I clicked the first app and began setting it up. What did I want my handle to be? I thought about it for a few minutes. This was a big decision.

I considered a bunch of different names like Jdavidson14. I always used the number fourteen because that was my birthday, January 4th. Then I thought about Buttonsguy14 or Butts4life14. After going through dozens of different names, I settled on JDButtons14. It was simple but effective.

My profile didn't take very long to set up. I chose a profile picture of Buttons and me, the same one that was the background of my phone. I started friending everyone from school. The first request I sent was to

Brad. He was my best friend and I wanted him to be my first friend online, too.

While I was following more and more people, there was a knock on my door. "Hey, squirt, can I come in?" Dad was at my door. I guess he was checking in on why I was up this late. It was already past one in the morning.

"Uh, yeah, Dad. Come on in!" I hid my phone under my pillow. Dad tried to open the door, but I quickly realized I'd never unlocked it. I walked over to the door and let him in.

"What's going on, big guy?" Dad asked. "It's a school night, pal. You're not even in your jammies."

"I know, I know. I'm sorry. Buttons and I were just hanging out. I'm having trouble falling asleep," I said.

"All right, well, you have school tomorrow. Get some shut-eye, will ya?" He hugged me and went down the hallway back to his bedroom.

I shut the door, but this time I didn't lock it. I didn't expect either of my parents to come back tonight, so I thought the coast was clear. I leaped back into bed and pulled my phone out from underneath the pillow. There was a notification. My first notification.

"Ghost has started following you."

Chapter 9

Brad and Sara got really close over the weekend. They texted more than usual and even went for a short walk together in the neighborhood. At one point, they both uploaded a picture of the two of them and their dogs. They really seemed to be hitting it off.

School went by pretty quickly on Monday. Jessie showed up with his new phone, oozing with confidence. Not only that, but most kids in school immediately took a new liking to him. Jessie was a great guy once you got to know him. But before he got his phone, no one had really given him a chance. It was hard to be an eighth-grade kid sometimes. It was all about the phone, all about the likes and the social media posts. If you couldn't participate or speak the same technological language, the reality was that you found yourself on the outside looking in. Brad felt bad for

Jessie, but at the same time, he needed to worry about himself.

"Hey, Brad," Sara said. She had snuck up behind him while he was at his locker.

Brad was standing with Jessie, who was looking down at his phone. "Oh, Sara. Hey! You caught me off guard, sorry," Brad said.

"Oh, sorry about that. I tend to be quiet." The two of them stood silently for a moment. Brad thought how funny it was that you could be so close with someone over the phone or on social media but have so little to talk about in person.

"Nice day out," Brad said.

"It sure is! I can't wait to walk Minnie later. I want to take her to the park." Minnie was Sara's chihuahua. She was six years old and weighed no more than five pounds, but she was a tiny ball of love. Sara loved her Minnie very much.

"Hey, that's a great idea," Brad said. "I should take Maxwell to the park, too!" Maxwell was Brad's four-year-old Golden Retriever.

The two stood in silence again for a moment before Brad responded. "Do you want to walk them together, maybe?"

Sara immediately smiled. *Finally*, she thought. "I'd love to! What do you say we meet at the corner of Eighty-Sixth Street at five thirty?" Sara figured that was early enough that it would still be light out and they could be home for dinner.

"That's perfect! I'll see you then!"

Brad and Jessie walked home together, as usual. Jessie stared down at his phone most of the time, looking at who knows what, and Brad was distracted by his daydreams about Sara. He left Jessie at the corner of 86th Street and zipped home quickly. He was nervous. He was starting to develop a serious crush on Sara.

Brad met up with Sara at the corner of 86th Street, as planned. Minnie ran up to Maxwell, and they did what dogs do. They sniffed each other's butts and were very playful. The two made quite an interesting pairing. Maxwell weighed over seventy pounds, and Minnie was absolutely tiny compared to him. Maxwell was a classic Golden and loved everything and everyone. Minnie was more of a sassy girl, often barking at strangers. They were an odd couple, but it worked. They got along well.

The same could be said about Sara and Brad. An unlikely duo, but the two of them seemed to work well. He had been talking about her to Jessie since the third grade. If not for his cell phone, he may never have had his first kiss.

Brad and Sara walked onward with their dogs. Brad quickly realized that talking to Sara in school and on his phone was a totally different experience from hanging out with her for longer than just a minute. They spoke about the most random things, like what color sheets they had on their beds and how they liked school lunch that day. It was kind of awkward, but they both enjoyed the company. The important thing was that they were awkward together. And that was okay by them.

The dogs were enjoying the company just as much. Brad and Sara had to keep pulling them away from each other. At one point, Minnie rode on top of Maxwell for a minute. Both of their tongues were lolling out.

Brad was the first to share his feelings. The more they walked together, the better the conversation got. He built up his courage.

"I think I really like you, Sara." He'd said it. The words were out. It was up to her now to decide what she wanted to do about it. Brad did hope she liked the words because it had taken so much of his energy to spit them out.

"I think I really like you, too, Brad." Sara felt the nervous tension in Brad. Although she was nervous, too, she'd known all along that Brad liked her. His declaration did not come as a shock. But she did like it.

Minnie and Maxwell lay down next to each other and stared at the humans as if they were wondering what was going to happen next. Tongues out, eyes gazing.

Sara grabbed Brad's hand. He was lost in shock. Brad had never held a girl's hand that wasn't his mom's before. He was immediately filled with butterflies.

Brad knew that Sara really did like him. She wasn't just saying it so she wouldn't make him feel bad. She actually meant her words, and that gave him just the courage he needed.

Brad held Sara's hand, leaned in, and gave her a kiss

on the lips—both of their first kisses. It was quick but effective. Both Brad and Sara were stunned. Happily stunned. The dogs seemed excited, too. They started barking loudly and spinning around in circles.

The two walked back through the park with their dogs, hand in hand. They were so happy to be with each other and not on their phones. Come to think of it, neither had even looked at their phone in the past hour or so. That was different for the two of them, in a good way. They wanted the walk to go on forever, but it was a school night and they both needed to get home.

Brad couldn't stop thinking about how he wanted to kiss Sara again. It was magical. He never knew he could feel so good about something. On that night, everything was perfect.

For whatever reason, his mind wandered to Jessie, which made him feel kind of bad. The walk he was taking with Sarah was the walk he normally did with Jessie. He'd kind of replaced Jessie that day. But he shouldn't feel bad about liking a girl, should he? He decided it wasn't as big a deal as he was making it out to be and that Jessie would totally be happy for him. The fact that he was even thinking about Jessie made him a great friend. Jessie was probably too occupied with his new phone to care, anyway. Everyone won.

Brad said goodbye to Sara with one more peck on the lips. Minnie and Maxwell ran up to each other and nuzzled their snouts as well.

Brad stood for a moment and watched Sara and

Minnie walk away. When they were out of view, Brad let out a big sigh of relief. It was over. He had done it—he had kissed Sara. He needed to tell Jessie. This was huge news. This was even bigger than Jessie finally getting a cell phone.

Brad took out his phone, but before he had a chance to text Jessie, he received a text message of his own.

STAY AWAY! OR DIE!

The sender's name was @Ghost.

Chapter 10

First, I tried texting Brad, but I didn't think he had service, because my messages weren't going through. Then I tried the walkies. "Brad, do you copy?" Nothing. No response. Where could he be? Brad never took this long to respond.

I decided that was my last attempt for the night. It was about nine thirty and I needed to go to bed. I wasn't angry, but I was certainly curious where he was. We normally talked every night, so this was odd.

Buttons nuzzled up next to me and I shut off my bedside lamp. I wasn't sure if I'd actually fallen asleep or not when Brad messaged me: *Dude, you need to see this. I'm scared.*

I picked up my phone and called him. It was too late for him to come over, but now that I had a cell phone, I wanted to use it every chance I had. Full-blown conversations on the walkies took forever.

Brad picked up after just one ring. He was talking so fast, it was hard to hear him.

"Dude, calm down. Relax. Start from the beginning," I said.

Brad slowed down and told me about the message.

"Someone has to be playing a trick on us, right?" I asked.

"I guess, man. I thought for sure this Ghost account was just spam, but now I'm starting to get worried," Brad responded.

I heard the grave concern in Brad's voice. He sounded frightened. Someone was messing with us. We had no idea who it was, but the message was direct, and it was scary.

It took me a few minutes to fully process what Brad had told me. We talked it out and tried to reason with each other. Who would actually want to threaten us? Did anybody have reason to dislike us? Things like that.

"What about Josh?" Brad said.

"It couldn't be Josh," I said.

I supposed it *could* have been Josh—we couldn't rule anyone out. But I didn't know why he would want to do anything like this.

"Why would Josh want to threaten us?" I said. "Sure, he ignores me often, but that doesn't make him dangerous."

"I suppose you're right," Brad said. "Do you have any other ideas?"

I thought for a few moments before I responded, and I wasn't really sure why I said what I said. The words just came out.

"I'll bet it was Sara."

There was silence on the other end.

"I bet she doesn't even like you and she's just getting close to you so she can set you up for an even bigger scare." *Did I really just say that?*

The words had come out of my mouth so quickly.

After some silence, Brad finally spoke. I thought he'd be angry, but he was quite relaxed.

"Dude, not cool. Why would you say something like that?"

I didn't have an answer for him. What I'd said was pretty mean and not like me. "I don't know, I'm sorry. It just came out. I don't think Sara did it."

"Actually …" Brad started. There was a change in his tone. Something was different now. It was like the tables were turned, and I could tell he was about to say something I wasn't going to like.

"There is something else I want to tell you," Brad continued, and I listened closely, carefully dissecting each word he said.

"I went for a walk with Sara tonight, and…"

I was starting to see where this was going, and anger built inside me. Brad had ditched me to go on a walk with Sara.

"… we kissed," Brad finished.

I was filled with rage. I shouldn't have been, but I

was. A good friend would've been happy for Brad. He'd just had his first kiss with a girl he had a huge crush on. But I was not at all happy for him. I was upset, and I lashed out at him.

"You ditched me! You jerk!" I shouted.

"Dude, I'm just being honest with you. You're the first person I'm telling about this," Brad said, calmly. He was clearly shocked by my reaction.

I thought about that, and it made sense. He was a good friend, but my anger wasn't going away.

"I'll tell you what—how 'bout you walk to school tomorrow with Sara?" I hung up.

What had I just done? Why was I so angry at Brad?

My phone immediately began ringing. Brad was calling. I let it go to voicemail several times before finally answering.

"Yes?" I said.

"Dude, I'm sorry for ditching you, but I really like Sara. It just kind of happened. You're my best friend." Brad's voice was genuine, and I knew he meant every word he said.

"I know, man. I know. I'm sorry for getting angry. I don't know what got into me. I've never felt like that before. It just kind of came out of me. Almost as if it wasn't even me speaking. I'm mostly happy for you, to be honest." My rage had subsided, but something still didn't feel right. I felt uneasy.

We both laughed before Brad spoke. "So, can we walk together tomorrow?"

"Of course," I responded.

That night, my mind raced with all kinds of weird thoughts and dreams. I didn't remember much, only that I woke in the middle of the night in a pool of sweat. My bed was so sweaty that Buttons was even slightly wet. I stood up and went to look in the mirror. My head was pounding. I turned on the lights and didn't like what I saw. I looked paler than usual. My eyelids seemed dark and heavy. I had small bags under my eyes. Maybe I was getting sick. I wiped my face with a towel and got back into bed. I looked at my phone. There were no notifications.

I woke up the next morning feeling better. My head still hurt, but not badly like it had last night, and the bags under my eyes were gone. I met Brad at the corner of 86th Street, as usual. I spoke first.

"Hey, man. I'm sorry again about last night. I don't know what got into me." I was sincere in my apology.

"Dude, ain't no sweat, brother. It's in the past. Let's just forget it ever happened," Brad said.

It made me feel good knowing that Brad could

forgive me for being an idiot.

"So, I need to know. Sara. The kiss. How was it?" I looked at him expectantly. Brad's kiss was huge news. I had to know the details.

"You know when you wake up on a Saturday morning, and you know you have the whole weekend left? And then Buttons comes up and starts licking your face, and you realize that for the next forty-eight hours, you don't have a care in the world? Plus the smell of ice cream and roses?" Brad continued on with the metaphors for a while.

"Yes, yes, and yes," I responded.

"Oh, well, all of that. Plus heaven." The two of us laughed.

"Morning, Geno," I said.

"Ey, my boys! What's shakin'? The usual?" Geno called out to us.

"You betcha," I said.

And as Geno was handing us our breakfast, he said, "Hey, Jessie, my man. You don't look so hot this morning."

"Yeah, I know. Thanks for pointing it out. I didn't sleep great last night," I said.

Geno had a weird look on his face. A worried look. "All right, man. Take it easy, okay? A thirteen-year-old shouldn't be so stressed."

"Appreciate the advice. We'll catch you on the flip," I said.

We walked away eating our sandwiches and Brad

continued to tell me about Sara and the kiss. He went on and on about how amazing it was, how she was as sweet as a jellybean. It was quite embarrassing, really. I had to laugh at how ridiculous he sounded.

We made it to school, but before we got to first period, things took a turn for the worse. Mostly for Brad.

We walked in the building, and immediately all eyes were staring at us. It seemed like every kid we walked by gave us a long, hard look. Then they looked down at their phones, then back up at us. Then came the laughter. We were clearly missing something.

We walked into Miller's first-period science class early. Miller was sitting in the corner of the room, facing his laptop. He was sitting completely upright, back straight, eyes locked on his computer. Josh and Nelson were huddled over their phones by Josh's desk. Marcus Sneadleman was laughing alone at his desk. The whole class was looking at something.

Before Brad had a chance to do so, I took out my phone. I had ninety-four notifications. *I didn't post anything,* I thought. *This is weird.* I opened up my Instagram and discovered there was a video uploaded from my profile. I clicked on it and was shocked to see what it was. It was a video of Brad confessing his love for Sara, describing her as waking up on a Saturday morning with your dog licking your face and the whole weekend ahead of you, plus ice cream, roses, and heaven.

I looked over at Brad, who had also realized what was happening. He didn't lift his gaze away from his phone. He looked like he was about to cry. But before I had a chance to explain anything to him—not that I had an explanation—Miller spoke.

"All right, ladies and gentlemen. At this point, all cell phones and technology should be put away. If I see it, it's mine. Now, let's begin."

Chapter 11

The moment Miller's class ended, Brad stormed away without waiting for me. I walked quickly to try and catch up to him, but he wouldn't stop.

"Dude, wait up!" He didn't answer me.

Why would he? He obviously thought I'd uploaded the video to embarrass him, but I hadn't. My phone must have been hacked, or maybe it was a complete accident somehow. I hadn't even recorded the video!

"Brad! Let me explain!" But Brad kept running until he was out of sight. I stood there in the hallway, trying to plan my next move. My mind was racing a million miles an hour. I tried to find a reasonable explanation as to how the video had gotten uploaded to social media, but I couldn't think of anything.

I tried to catch up with Brad several times throughout the day, but he ignored me every time.

Even at lunch, he sat alone. When I went up to him, he picked up his tray and walked away. Even though I had my phone and the numbers of everyone in school, I had never felt more alone.

Over the course of the day, the video that I had seemingly uploaded got more popular by the minute. The comments were getting out of hand, too. I thought about taking it down to appease Brad and show him that it was an accident. But part of me was loving this popularity. For once, I was getting the credit and attention.

I could only imagine what Sara must have been thinking. She must have been mortified by this. I knew she liked him and all but being put on blast like this was a whole different story. People getting an inside look at her and Brad's relationship had to be a nightmare. I felt terrible.

After the eighth-period bell rang and school was over, I took one last shot at talking to Brad. I walked over to his locker, but when I rounded the corner, I saw him talking to Sara. The two of them were standing face-to-face. Their cheeks were red, both clearly embarrassed by the whole situation. I couldn't make out most of what they were saying, but they were loud enough so I could hear that *something* was being said.

There was a moment of silence, and then Sara stepped closer to Brad and kissed him on the lips. She followed the kiss with a hug. Unbelievable. *This is a good thing, right?* I thought. If they weren't mad at each other, all would be well. Brad would have to forgive me now.

I walked up to them and played dumb. "Hey, guys! What's going on?"

Sara looked at me without saying a word. She stared me down as she walked away.

Brad paused before he spoke to me angrily. "Dude, how are you going to pretend like nothing happened?"

"Well, I tried to get hold of you all day to explain, but you wouldn't even talk to me!" I replied.

I just wanted Brad to hear me out. I knew that what had happened *seemed* to be my fault, but it wasn't! I hadn't done anything wrong. I would never have embarrassed my best friend. This was a misunderstanding and a total accident. I knew how much he liked Sara, and I was happy for him.

"Okay, then, let's hear it," Brad said. He wanted the raw details.

I thought for several moments before responding. All day I'd been trying to catch up to him and explain what had happened, but in that moment it hit me that I didn't really *know* what had happened. There was no real explanation for it.

"This is going to sound crazy, but I need you to hear me out," I said.

"Okay. Out with it." Brad already seemed like he didn't have the time for what I had to say.

"I didn't upload that video." I spoke with a serious tone. I needed Brad to truly understand my words. I knew I sounded like an idiot, but I was telling the truth. "I don't know what happened, but you were with me this morning. I never even took my phone out to take a video of you. It was in my pocket the whole time."

"That doesn't make any sense. You must have done it when I wasn't looking," Brad said.

"No, I swear! I need you to believe me. Have I ever lied to you before? I don't know what happened! Maybe the phone was recording through my pants pocket. I really don't know, but this is a big misunderstanding. I did not take that video. I feel terrible, and I would never embarrass you like this on purpose." I desperately wanted his forgiveness.

"That's it? That's your whole story? No explanation or anything? You expect me to believe you, just like that?" Brad was not buying it.

As I was about to respond, Marcus Sneadleman walked by. I smelled him coming; he smelled like dirt and body odor. He was wearing the same brown pants and plain black T-shirt he always wore. His glasses hung half off his face.

"Nice video, Davidson! Killer watch!" Then he blew a kiss at Brad, mocking him. "Say hi to Sara for me!"

I didn't even have a chance to respond. Brad slammed his locker shut, and as he walked away, I stood there alone.

I took out my phone, and again, I had a zillion notifications. The video had over seven hundred views. I didn't even know seven hundred people!

I walked home by myself. The whole walk, I kept my phone tucked away. I had wanted a phone so badly, and although I loved having it, it was already causing me so much trouble.

I knew accidents happened, and that was all this was. A big accident, a big misunderstanding. I just hoped Brad would eventually forgive me. I hadn't done it on purpose, and nothing like this would ever happen again. He just wasn't seeing clearly because he was so hurt. And I understood that.

I got home, and Buttons was waiting for me in the doorway. "Hey, buddy." He ran up to me, his tail wagging furiously back and forth. I bent down to pet him and he licked my face all over. At least Buttons appreciated me.

"Mom? Dad?" There was no response. "Hello? Anyone home?" Again, there was no response. They must've been out. I walked into the kitchen, and there was a note.

Dear Squirt,

Mom and I went out to meet your aunt and uncle for dinner. Mom left you some pasta in the fridge. All you need to do is heat it up in the microwave. Be back around ten-ish. CALL US ON OUR CELL IF YOU NEED ANYTHING!

Love,
Dad and Mom

It was not like them to be out on a weekday. But then again, weird things were happening quite often lately. I opened the fridge and saw the unappetizing meal they'd left for me. The sauce was hardened into a dark red mush. I decided to pass. I checked the pantry for any worthwhile snacks to munch on. Also not much.

Buttons stood next to me, staring up at me with glassy eyes.

"Oh, sorry, bud." My mind had been so all over the place that I'd almost forgotten to feed Buttons. He scarfed down his kibble and his whole bowl of water in moments.

I threw my schoolbag onto the floor and sat down at the kitchen table. I took out my phone and saw that I had a text message from Nelson Strong:

Dude, that video of Brad today was pure gold!

I thought about all the times Nelson hadn't been as nice to me as I was to him. He was never directly mean to me, but he'd never given me the time of day. I'd always felt like he thought I was beneath him for some reason. Now that I had a cell phone, everyone seemed to be treating me differently, including Brad. It wasn't always in a good way.

I thought for a few minutes before responding. I had always tried so hard to be friends with people like Nelson and Josh, but they'd never treated me well.

Now, all of a sudden, I had a chance to get closer with them. It felt weird, but at the same time, it felt good. People were giving me attention. Kids at school were seeking me out. I was becoming popular. And besides, Brad wasn't talking to me, so what was the worst that could happen? Maybe I needed to make some new friends.

I responded.

Ha ha, thanks, dude! Those two lovebirds deserve each other! They also kinda make me sick.

And I finished the text off with a barf emoji.

Nelson and I texted back and forth for a while. He was actually a funny guy. The conversation ended with him inviting me to the party at Josh's house Friday night. *Wow, a real party*, I thought. I wondered if Sara was invited. And for that matter, if Brad was.

I wanted to reach out to him and ask, but he was probably still mad at me. I'd tried to reason with him earlier in the day, hadn't I? I wasn't my fault he didn't want to believe me about the video. I kind of felt bad about talking to Nelson, so I tried convincing myself it was okay. Deep down inside, I knew it wasn't right, but talking to Nelson had felt good. Talking badly about Brad and Sara had also kind of felt good. It seemed like I was getting more popular by the second, and that was awesome.

My mind was racing through everything that

happened today. Between the video, the fight with Brad, and now the texting with Nelson and the party, my thoughts were a blur. So much had happened. I started to develop a small headache and decided I needed some sleep. I went upstairs to lay down, and Buttons followed me.

Before I made it into my bed, I noticed something in the bathroom mirror as I walked by. Something odd that I had never seen before. On my neck, there was a patch of skin that looked different. It was greenish brown and felt a little bumpy.

WEIRD, I thought. *Must be a rash.*

But the events of the day were weighing on my mind too heavily to really care.

Chapter 12

The talk of the town at school on Friday was Josh's party. Now that I was invited, it felt like a whole new world had opened up. Brad wouldn't talk to me, but I didn't mind as much anymore, because everyone else was talking to me now. Nelson and Josh texted me all day to make sure I was coming to the party. It was like we had been best friends forever. I had never realized how funny they were. The three of us started our own group chat and filled it with all kinds of jokes and gossip about other kids in school. They brought up Brad a few times, most notably the video of him confessing his love for Sara. I hesitated slightly when joking about it, but why should I care anymore? It was he who had walked out on me, not the other way around. If he were really my best friend, he would care more. Josh and Nelson were my new best friends, and

Brad would have to deal with that.

In Miller's class, I looked over at Brad a few times. I tried to get his attention just to say hi, at least. But he never looked at me once. When the final bell rang, he walked right on out, just like he had the day before.

"Yo, J-man!" Josh came up as we were leaving class and put his arm around me. I stared at Brad as he walked out the door.

"Yo, J-man right back atcha!" That sounded boring. Nonetheless, Josh laughed.

"Tonight is going to be so killer!" Josh said.

"Yeah, man, thanks for inviting me. I'm excited to come hang," I said.

"As if I wasn't going to invite you!" Josh said.

Josh was acting like we had talked every day for years. It kind of rubbed me the wrong way, but I guess that came with the territory of starting new friendships.

"So, I was thinking we should definitely order pizza. Pizza is a must, but what kind of snacks should we do? Any suggestions? Oh yeah, and we have to watch a movie, so maybe popcorn is a good idea …"

Josh went on for a while before letting me get a word in. And then when I did talk, it felt like he was barely listening. Talking to him was kind of like talking to a wind-up doll. He kept going and going until his string ran out, and then he just stared off into the distance. I felt like I had to check him to see if he was awake.

"I think I have some popcorn at my house, so I'll

bring it over," I said.

Josh was making the smallest things into such a big deal, but I told myself he just wanted to make sure everyone had a good time at his house.

"J-man, thanks! That's a huge help, big dawg!" Josh said energetically.

I appreciated his gratitude, but I really hadn't offered to do too much. It was like he was trying to impress me. That was something I had never experienced before. All of a sudden, I was so cool to him. I liked it, but at the same time, it felt a little fake. *I might as well ride this wave*, I thought.

We made small talk about the party for a little while longer, then said our goodbyes and said we would catch up later on social media before the party.

"Definitely text me later, bro! Check out my Insta before the party, too—it's going to be rad!" Josh said.

I could only imagine what Josh was going to post about. I pictured him and Nelson in front of a mirror, checking themselves out, blasting music, getting ready for half the school to show up.

I left school by myself to feed and walk Buttons. I went through my usual after-school routine all alone. No Brad.

I thought about texting him to apologize, but every time, I reminded myself that this whole thing wasn't my fault. I hadn't even done anything wrong! Why should I be the one to cave and apologize? If he was my real friend, shouldn't he believe what I'd said about the video? It wasn't me who'd posted it. My camera had probably just gone on in my pocket. It was just an accident. Josh had to understand that. But he didn't. Not yet, at least.

I wondered if Sara was going to be at the party. I knew now that both Brad and Sara were invited, but I doubted Brad would go. He was really freaking out about the whole video thing.

And then, as if things weren't bad enough already between Brad and me, Josh posted a video that made me think Brad would really never talk to me again.

About an hour before the party, Nelson and Josh posted a video pretending to be Brad and Sara, completely making fun of them. Josh pretended to be Brad and Nelson pretended to be Sara. Josh basically re-enacted Brad's comments confessing his love for Sara, and then Nelson pretended to kiss Josh! By the end of the video, the two of them were laughing like hyenas. They couldn't stop.

My stomach dropped. Why would they do that?

I wanted to be friends with them, but I didn't want Brad or Sara to get hurt. I felt terrible, but I didn't know how to respond.

Brad wouldn't talk to me, and that was okay, I guess. But Josh and Nelson were crossing the line. I wanted to stand up for Brad and say something to them, but what would happen then? Would they start bullying me and make videos mocking me? I didn't want that, either.

I decided to play it cool and see what happened.

Brad was not going to be at the party. Maybe it would all blow over. The whole topic would probably die out shortly. After all, what was everyone's obsession with Brad and Sarah, anyway? Why did they want to be involved in their relationship?

I got ready for the party and headed downstairs. Mom and Dad were sitting at the kitchen table.

"Hey, squirt! Where ya off to?" I realized that my parents had no idea what was going on. Not about the cell phone, not about Brad, not about any of it.

"Oh, I, uh—I'm going to Josh's party." I was honest.

"Well, that sounds fun. Who is Josh again?" Mom asked.

"Josh Hartley, from school," I said.

"That's great, squirt! Have a rockin' time! I'm guessing you need a lift?"

"No thanks, Dad. I'm going to walk. It's only a few blocks away." Josh lived on 83rd Street between 1st and 2nd Avenues.

"All right, well, be safe, and if you need anything, use Brad's phone and call us."

"Yup, will do, Mom," I said.

Of course, I wouldn't be anywhere near Brad's phone. I had no idea where Brad would be. Brad and I hadn't spoken in twenty-four hours. But I couldn't tell Mom that because then she would start asking questions, and it would lead back to my cell phone.

I left the house and started my walk to Josh's

apartment. The video they'd posted was getting all kinds of activity. People were loving it.

I thought about commenting. But what would I even say? I wanted to fit in, to not let Josh and Nelson down, but at the same time I didn't want to hurt Brad. I decided not to comment or even like the video. If either of them asked me about it, I'd say I didn't have a chance to check it out. They would believe me, right?

I rang the doorbell to Josh's apartment. He opened the door with Nelson and a girl from school, Isabella Rodney. I didn't even know she was friends with Josh or Nelson. I guess I really was out of the loop for a long time.

"J-man! Welcome, *welcome*!" And as Josh spoke, he brought me in for a big hug, and then Nelson and Isabella joined us.

I heard a ton of voices in the distance. His apartment was huge. It was three floors, and there were so many rooms. The decor was fancy-shmancy. We walked through the entryway and past the kitchen, where there was food everywhere. Pizza, chips, chocolate, soda. This was incredible.

"Is your mom home?" I asked.

"Yup! She loves when I have people over. It makes her feel 'young again,' she always says. But she's upstairs with Dad. Don't even worry about them," Josh said.

We continued on into a large living room. I was shocked by how many people were there—at least twenty-five, but maybe more. I didn't even know most of them. Many of them I recognized from school, but I didn't remember their names. I recognized Cindy Liu from class, and Margot Daniels. Again, I had no idea any of these people were friends with Josh and Nelson. Maybe I had always been *so* on the outside that I just hadn't realized it? It felt like I was being initiated into an underground cult. I was waiting for them to ask me to perform a secret handshake.

I realized in that moment that this was, like, a real party, and I had never been to an actual real party before. I instantly became nervous. *How do I act? Who should I talk to?* I wanted Brad back. This didn't feel right to me. But at the same time, it felt *so* right.

"Davidson, welcome to La Casa de Hartley!" Josh introduced me to a few of the kids from school who I didn't know. He showed me around for a few minutes, and then we plopped down on the couch. There were also bowls of snacks on the table in this room.

The next thing I noticed was in the center of the room. It was so big that it should have been the very first thing I laid eyes on. Now I couldn't tear my gaze away.

Right smack-dab in the middle of the room was the biggest TV I had ever seen.

Josh noticed me looking at his mondo TV. "You like that?" he asked as he put his arm around me.

"Um, yes?" I responded. "How big is that thing?! Holy moly."

"It's a ninety-nine-inch HDTV, my amigo," Josh said as I continued to stare. "Parents just picked it up a few weeks ago. As soon as they got it, I knew I needed to have people over. Just wait until we turn it on."

I was so impressed with everything at Josh's party. The people, the food, the entertainment. This was epic. I was finally in. I had made it. I was part of the popular crowd.

This was exactly what I had always wanted. And yet, for some reason, something still felt off. Why did I find myself thinking about Brad when I was at this incredible party with half the kids from school?

I looked around and tried to see if I could spot Sara, or even Rachel. I figured that if Sara came without Brad, it was probably going to be with Rachel. I couldn't find either of them.

"By the way, dude, *loved* your comment on our video!" And as Josh spoke, Nelson came up behind him and chimed in.

"Jessie, I don't know why we never noticed it before, but you are the man! We love what you're doing these days. Keep the fire coming, man! Love the comments and love your creativity!"

The only problem was, I didn't know what comment he was talking about. I had specifically chosen *not* to like or comment on the video.

I opened my phone and went straight to Instagram. Josh's video had a ridiculous amount of likes and comments. I realized quickly most of them were replies to something I'd written. The only problem was that I hadn't written anything.

There it was: a comment from me, from @JDButtons14. It said:

"BRAVO, BRAVO. This should be up for performance of the year! You guys look exactly like them. A bunch of losers!"

Oh, no. No no no. This isn't happening. My heart dropped into my stomach. I checked the username again to make sure my eyes weren't playing tricks on me. But there it was, staring back at me: @JDButtons14. My username, and my comment.

I didn't write this. What is happening?

Before I even had a chance to gather my thoughts, as this was all crashing down on me, Josh stood up on the couch and made an announcement.

"Attention, all! Firstly, I'd like to thank everyone for showing up to my party tonight. Please don't hesitate to help yourself to the food and drinks. Without further ado, I'd like to bring your attention to the beautiful screen you see before you. Feast your eyes."

I was having a hard time processing what was happening. I felt like I'd swallowed my Adam's apple. My throat was dry, my lips numb. The hairs on my arms were standing up and I had goose bumps popping up all over my body.

The massive television screen turned on. For a moment, the screen was blue, then black, and then an image finally appeared. Josh was playing the video he had posted to Instagram. But within moments, a different video appeared.

Josh was standing there in his underwear. He was in front of a mirror combing his hair. He was singing "The Wheels on the Bus Go Round and Round." Besides the fact that his voice was laughably bad, everyone could see his entire body, practically naked.

The entire party went silent. No one said a word. We just watched in awe as Josh continued to sing the song in his underwear. Then people started to look around the room at each other and whisper. Then came the giggles, then laughter. Josh was still silent, his eyes fixed on the video, which was now repeating on the big screen. I noticed a tear roll down his cheek.

He turned around to look at me, then picked up something off of the projector. I noticed he had grabbed a cell phone. I grabbed at my pockets to ensure it was not mine, but my phone wasn't there. How had my phone gotten all the way over by the projector?

It was clear for everyone to see. With tears streaming down his face and laughter surrounding him, Josh looked at me.

The video on the projector was being broadcast directly from my cell phone.

Chapter 13

"How could you do this to me?" Josh said. "I thought we were friends!" Then he began shouting. "GET OUT!"

Josh's fury raged through the entire living room. No one else moved or even blinked. Their eyes were fixed on what was happening. "I don't ever want to see you again. Don't talk to me, don't come near me. I HATE YOU!"

And with those words, Josh launched my phone across the living room and down the hall, past the kitchen and toward the front door.

I ran out of the living room. The silence was deafening as I grabbed my phone before leaving. It was shattered. The screen was completely cracked in what seemed like every spot. The camera had a huge split right down the middle. *Excellent. I finally get a phone and just like that, it's gone. Poof.*

Although it was destroyed, the screen was still working. *A good sign … I guess.*

I put the phone in my pocket and ran home as fast as I could. My mind was a blur. I had felt alone before—very alone—but now I felt alone and scared. I didn't know what to do or where to go. I wanted Brad. I *needed* Brad. He was my best friend. Why was all of this happening? Ever since I'd gotten this phone, weird things had started happening.

When I walked in, my parents were still sitting at the kitchen table. "Well, that was quick, sport," Dad said.

"Yeah, the party was boring," I said.

I didn't say another word and dashed upstairs to my room. Buttons followed behind me.

"Okay…" I began talking to myself, pacing back and forth. "What should I do?" I needed to contact Brad. I looked over at Buttons who was laying on his back, sprawled out. I didn't know what to do, but I did know that Brad would be able to help. He was always able to help. And the only thing that was clear to me right then was that I needed to get him back immediately.

First, I tried to reach him on the walkies. "Brad, are you there? Do you copy? This is an emergency. I need you, man. Please pick up. I know you're there." There was silence on the other end.

"Brad, it's Jessie. Please, if you're there, pick up." I tried a second and third time, but I still got nothing but silence in return.

"Brad," I said. "Listen, I apologize for the way I've been acting and for the video being uploaded. You are my best friend, and you don't deserve any of this. You are the only person on this planet who could ever be my best friend. I'm not sure what's going on right now, but I need you. I'm alone and scared, and I have no one else to go to. Please, Brad. If you are there, answer me." A tear started to form in the corner of my eye.

The static was deafening until a whispered voice came through.

"What do you want?" Brad said.

I could tell from the tone in his voice that he was not going to let me off easy, but at least he had answered. I let out a huge sigh of relief and wiped the tear from my eye.

"Brad, oh man." Another feeling of pure relief washed over me. "Thank you for responding. I need to talk to you. Something weird is going on."

"Speak. I'm listening." Brad's tone remained unchanged.

"I need to talk to you in person," I responded.

"No. Anything you need to tell me, you can say here. I don't want to see you," Brad said.

"Brad, please. I can't do this over the walkies. There is something going on, something I can't explain. I can't do this alone. Please," I pleaded to my best friend, hoping for a chance.

There was a long pause before Brad responded. "If this is another joke, I'm never going to speak—"

I cut him off. "Brad, you are my best friend. I didn't upload that video, I swear it. I need you to come over right now," I cried out in desperation.

There was another long pause before he responded. "Stay there, I'll be over in a few."

Soon Brad arrived, and I began pleading my case.

"Okay, first of all, I'm sorry. I need you to know that. I didn't mean for you to get hurt." I hesitated, then kept going. "I know I apologized before, but I wanted to do it in person. You didn't deserve that kind of treatment. I know it must have been embarrassing for Sara, too. She didn't deserve that either. I don't even know how it happened, but I'm sorry. Somehow it must've been my fault, and I'm sorry."

Deep down, I knew it wasn't my fault, but there was no other excuse to be made. The video had been uploaded by my account somehow. And for that, I needed to apologize.

Brad stared back at me. His arms were folded across his chest.

"I forgive you," he said.

An immediate wave of relief came over me.

"But it's going to take a lot more than that for Sara to forgive you. She's *not happy*. Your video wasn't even the worst of it. We both saw your comments on Josh and Nelson's video."

All this time I'd been worried about how Brad was feeling, but Sara was involved too. I wondered what everyone must have been thinking about her.

"Brad. I didn't write those comments and I didn't upload that video of you confessing your feelings. I need you to believe me. I swear it." I spoke with purpose.

"All right, fine. I get it. You didn't mean to upload the video. It was an accident, I know. But how do you explain how these comments magically appeared on Josh's video?" Brad answered.

"I can't explain it, that's the problem. I don't know what's happening, Brad. But I do know I didn't write those comments! All these weird things have been happening lately," I said.

I told Brad about the party, start to finish. About how Josh and Nelson were treating me like I was their best friend, about all the people who were there, about the food.

"I don't understand his problem. What did Sara and I ever do to him?" Brad was upset, and so was I.

"I know, man, I know. I feel terrible about it. Also, you need to know that I didn't write that comment. You have to believe me. Something is going on with my phone. It's broken or something," I said.

I spoke without thinking. There was no way Brad was going to believe me, but I was telling the truth. What else was I supposed to do? I needed to come clean and tell him everything. After that, I could only hope for the best.

"I know you didn't," Brad said.

My ears perked up at his words. It was like a huge

weight was lifted off me.

"You're a good friend, Jessie. You're my best friend. If you tell me you didn't write it, I believe you," Brad said.

Excitedly, I began speaking a mile a minute. I continued on about the party, finishing off with the giant TV screen Josh had in his living room and how my phone had somehow projected the video of him singing in his underwear.

"Let me get this straight. In this video, Josh was singing in front of his mirror?" Brad asked.

"That's correct." I responded.

"And he was in his underwear?"

"That is also correct." I was laughing as I spoke.

"And everyone at the party saw it?" Brad was smiling now, too.

"Correct, correct, and correct!" The two of us were laughing together now. It felt good. I had missed my best friend quite a bit.

I had forgotten until that very moment that Josh had launched my phone across the room and shattered it. It had still been working when I'd left the party, but something in me wished it wasn't.

"And then everyone just stood there and stared at Josh. I couldn't believe it. He was crying! I felt terrible, but he also kind of deserved it!" The two of us were laughing even harder now.

"Dude, that is classic. Seems like he got a taste of his own medicine. Maybe he'll stop treating others so poorly. I can't wait to tell Sara about this," Brad said.

"So then he threw my phone all the way down this long hallway toward the door, yelling at me to get out. It's totally shattered. It cracked everywhere. Even the camera split down the middle," I said.

I was overcome with relief about my phone breaking. Having Brad back helped me understand that I was actually starting to really dislike it.

"Oh, I'm sorry to hear that, Jess. I know how badly you wanted it."

"No, don't be. It was causing me so much stress. There's something not quite right about it. Something off, something weird," I said.

Brad took out his phone to text Sara and tell her what had happened. I was feeling great. It felt good not to worry about my phone and social media. I was relaxed; I wasn't thinking about my next video upload or what everyone would say about it. And Brad was with me, which was most important.

I thought maybe it would be a good idea to get rid of the phone. The screen was cracked, and I doubted it would still take good pictures.

I pulled it out of my pocket and shrieked at what I saw. There was my phone. The very same phone that Josh had launched across the room. The very same phone whose screen was shattered earlier that night. But now the screen was perfectly smooth, the camera shiny and glossy. No cracks, no lines. It was even cleaner than it was before.

Chapter 14

"Brad…" I said. "Brad, the screen was broken. I saw it with my own eyes."

I stared at the phone in my hand, mesmerized. How could this be? Just a little while ago, Josh had thrown my phone onto a hardwood floor, and it had cracked everywhere. And now the phone looked like it was brand new, never used before.

"There is something terrible about this phone, Brad. I need you to believe me," I said.

Brad looked at the phone, too. He had a peculiar look on his face. He realized how serious I was.

Brad thought about the situation for a moment, then responded, "Okay, so let's be clear about a few things. First of all, you're telling me the truth, correct?"

If I were Brad, I would probably be asking the same question. I definitely sounded crazy, and I almost didn't believe it myself!

"I swear it. I don't have a rational explanation for it, but I'm telling you the truth," I said.

Brad took the phone from my hand and examined it. First, he looked at the front screen, up and down. He smoothed it in between his hands. Then he flipped it over and reviewed the back and camera.

"Everything looks normal to me," Brad said.

Brad continued to look through the phone. He checked out the interface, the apps, the whole thing. It was exactly the same as every other phone in every way.

"I think I might have a solution." And with those words, Brad led me out the door.

I followed Brad down the block along what seemed like our normal route, except he stopped at the corner. "What are you doing?" I asked.

"You're telling me this phone is the reason for all of these problems, right?" Brad asked.

"Yes. I don't know how or why, but yes, it seems that way."

"Well, then, here's how we fix the problem." Brad lifted the phone with his right hand and dropped it into a trash can.

I didn't know how to respond. My first reaction was anger and resentment, but then I was flooded with relief. I looked down into the abyss of the garbage. The phone stared back at me.

"All this time, it was all I ever wanted," I whispered.

Brad put his arm around me. "Sometimes the things

we want most are the things that we can't have."

I didn't know exactly what that meant, but I agreed. I felt refreshed now that it was over. I would cut my losses and go back to my boring life. The thing I had started to understand was that boring was good. I had spent so much time desiring what others had, wanting and needing a cell phone, only to find out how much pain and stress having one caused me. It felt great to be free of it. No messages to check, no videos to upload. I felt calm and relaxed.

"I gotta get out of here, dude," Brad said. "I'm sorry you had to lose your phone. Whatever actually did happen, it's over."

"I'm sorry again. I don't ever want to see that phone again. My parents were right," I said.

We fist-bumped, and Brad walked back to his apartment. "Best buds for life."

I waited a few moments. Something kept me there. My eyes wandered back over to the garbage. The phone was still right there. I could see it on top of a newspaper. A voice inside my head was telling me to go back and take it. But I knew that I shouldn't.

I walked back up to the garbage can, the phone staring back at me. I picked it back up and brushed off the smudge of dirt that had gotten on the screen. The screen turned on, but the background that had been a picture of Buttons and me just minutes earlier was now a blank white palette of nothing. Maybe it was actually broken. I decided I didn't want to wait another second to find out what was wrong with it, if anything. I dropped it back into the garbage. It fell down to the bottom this time, where I couldn't see it. Good riddance.

I walked back home feeling great. I knew deep down inside that I had made the right choice. I had freed myself of that phone. I had Brad back, and things would return to the way they were before I got the phone. The other kids at school would ignore me, just the way I liked it.

I walked into my apartment super late. All the lights in the house were off. My parents must have gone to sleep. I made my way into the kitchen and immediately heard Buttons's tail wagging.

"Hey, buddy! Oh, I missed you tonight!" I bent down and he ran up to me. He was so happy to see me. He gave me a good face licking. "Thanks, buddy." I set him down and walked up to my room. Sleep came easy that night.

I woke to the sound of my walkie-talkie. "Come in. Jessie, are you there? It's almost eleven o'clock. Do you copy?"

I wiped away the slobber all over my face and picked up the walkie. "Yes, I'm here. I slept so late," I said.

"Copy that, sleepyhead. Heading to the park with Sara. Do you want to come with us?"

With Sara? And they wanted me to join? I thought that Sara hated me, but I guessed this would be a good time to apologize to her. I was sure Brad had spoken to her already and hopefully put in a good word.

"Sure, I'm down," I said. "Meet you at our spot in ten." I got out of bed, brushed my teeth, got dressed, and was ready to go.

Brad and Sara were waiting for me when I got there. "Hey, guys," I said.

I was slightly shy and even more embarrassed. I didn't really know Sara too well and hadn't spoken to her much in the past. I knew I was already on her hate list, so I didn't know how to act.

"Hi," Sara said.

Brad didn't say a word. He didn't even look at me. He stared down at his feet.

"Look, Sara, I'm sorry. I don't know what Brad told you, but there's something strange … in the neighborhood." *Did I just quote* Ghostbusters*? Really, Jessie?*

Sara looked confused. "Did you just quote *Ghostbusters*, Jessie?" She started laughing. "I can't even be mad—that was hilarious. Did you do that on purpose?" She was giggling as she spoke.

I laughed even harder. My accidental goofiness broke the ice just fine. Brad looked up from his feet. He joined the laughter.

"It's all right," Sara said. "You are Brad's best friend, so I know you're a good person." Her words made me so happy. "Whatever actually happened is in the past. I want us to be cool." The three of us shared a laugh and continued walking over to the park.

"I wish you guys could have seen Josh's face when that video was on the giant TV. Everyone just stared in silence. I couldn't believe it!" Both Brad and Sara were laughing hysterically.

"That's unbelievable!" Sara said. "How did you get that video on your phone?"

Brad and I stopped for a moment at that question. I didn't really know to respond, to be honest. I didn't have the answer for her.

"Sara, I know this is going to sound weird, but I don't know. I didn't even play it! One minute my phone was in my pocket, and the next, Josh was holding it in shock as it was playing the video," I said.

Sara knew the truth because Brad had told it to her. I guess she had a hard time believing it. Just like Brad did, and just like I did.

"Yeah, Brad mentioned that. I guess there was something wrong with that phone, huh?" she asked.

"Yeah, I guess so," I responded. "I'm just glad it's over and done with."

"Yeah, I never really liked Josh anyway," Sara said. "I was just kind of friends with him because it was the cool thing to do. Everyone seems to be friends with him, but nobody actually likes him. Except for Nelson, of course."

The three of us continued walking, and it felt easy. I was happy for Brad. It seemed like he and Sara were really clicking. They really liked each other. At one point, she even gave him a peck on the cheek, right in front of me.

We finished our walk and said our goodbyes. "See you guys in school tomorrow?" I said.

"Definitely!" Sara said.

"I'll hit you up later on the walkies," Brad responded. And with that, I went back home.

I walked in, expecting Buttons to come running up to me, tail wagging, tongue lolling out. But instead, he was barking. I didn't know where from, but I definitely heard it.

"Butts?" I called out. He just kept on barking. "Where are you, bud?" I looked around the kitchen first, but he was not there. The barking continued. Then I moved into the living room and dining room. Nothing. The barking went on as I walked upstairs and began checking the bedrooms.

"Hey, boy, come here. Come on, bud!" This seemed a little off to me. Buttons always greeted me at the front door. And if not, he was usually sleeping.

I entered my bedroom and found him at last.

"There's my big boy," I said, but I gaped in horror at what I saw when I approached him.

There it was, right on top of my dresser, next to my walkie.

Underneath my lamp was my cell phone.

Chapter 15

No. This can't be happening. I just threw it in the garbage can! I saw it with my own eyes!

Even though I had thrown the phone away, there it was. Right in front of me, as if it had never left. I wanted to scream and cry. I was filled with rage and many other emotions I didn't know how to process. How was this possible? This was a twisted joke! I picked it up, and again, the background was a picture of Buttons and me.

Would Brad even believe me this time if I told him what had happened? I thought I was probably running out of chances, but what else could I do? I didn't know who else to call or talk to. An instant headache surged through my head. Not just a simple brain-freeze-type headache but a sharp, migraine-like, unbearable pain. I was dizzy. If not for my bed, I would have smashed my head on the floor. I fell down onto my mattress and saw stars. The room was spinning.

I woke to a buzz. My phone was vibrating. Who could possibly be texting me now? Everyone at the party saw this phone shatter, and Brad thought it was at the bottom of a garbage can. I sat up. The splitting pain in my head was slightly better than when I had fainted, but it was still rough. I picked up my phone. The sender was Ghost. *This can't be happening.* The message said:

You can't escape us now. You will be ours forever!

I wanted to shatter my phone again. I wanted to smash it into a thousand pieces. I wanted to pack it up in a suitcase and send it on a plane to the farthest parts of the Earth, far away from New York City. But I was starting to understand that none of that would work. This phone wasn't an ordinary phone. There was something deeper, something stranger, something scarier happening.

In that moment, my stomach dropped and I felt sharp pains. My belly throbbing, I lifted my shirt and saw something horrible. My whole torso was green, brown and putrid! Plus, there was a weird and slimy goo all over. I ran over to the mirror and saw that the Jessie staring back at me was skin and bones. It looked like my body was shrinking down to nothing. Just a skeleton.

Through my headache, I thought about what to do.

Brad and Sara wouldn't believe me if I told them what was happening; they would probably think I was playing another joke on them. That was the last thing I wanted. I decided I needed to move forward by myself. I needed to go back to where this had all started. I needed to find the man who gave me the phone and give it back to him. And then I remembered the promise he'd forced out of me:

"Promise that you'll accept this gift from me, this cell phone. It's yours forever. But you may never *return it. You must keep it, and you may never give it back to me."*

I had agreed, but I hadn't signed a contract or anything. He had to take it back. He *had to!*

I tucked the phone into my pocket and put on a hoodie and my boots. I ran out the front door so fast, leaving Butts lying on the floor in sadness.

"I'll be back soon, buddy, I promise!" I said as I launched myself down the steps and out the front door.

I knew where I had to go and what I needed to do. I walked along Brad's and my usual route to the park. I must have passed out for several hours because it was dark out now, although I wished it wasn't. I entered the park and tried to retrace my steps exactly. With each step, I was more and more anxious. I couldn't think straight, but I knew this was the only way. I didn't have any other options. I needed to figure out what was actually going on, and the only person who could help me was the creepy old man who had given me the phone.

I was nearing the right spot in the park, so I looked for a sign, anything. When I had first discovered the man here, there was a lantern lighting a small clearing. I didn't see any lanterns this time, though. I searched endlessly, but I couldn't find him. I couldn't even find the clearing. I thought I had found the spot where he'd been, but there was nothing there. *It was right here! It has to be here!*

I ran in circles, and my emotions built up more and more. I began to cry, and I fell to the ground. My head was pounding worse than before now.

"HELP!" I screamed.

I doubted anyone could hear me, though. I was in the middle of the woods in Central Park in the middle of the night.

"Boy," a whispered voice said. I stood up and turned around. "Look at me, boy."

A man stood there. He was holding a lamp. He was young and muscular. His full head of black hair sat on top of a chiseled, pointy face.

The man spoke again. "Do you not recognize me, boy?"

Recognize him? I had never seen this man before, I was sure of it.

"Please, sir. You have to help me!" I started to tell him about my cell phone before he interrupted me.

"Boy! Enough! You do not need to explain to me the horrors of that cell phone. I am aware, for I am the very same man who gave it to you!"

I looked him directly in the face. I stared at his eyes. Those same green eyes. *No. It can't be.* Was it really him? I realized it was, only he was different. Before, he had looked like he was on his deathbed. He'd had wispy strings of hair on his bald, spotted head. Now he had a full head of thick black hair. Before, he'd had thin, bony, ancient skin covered in slime and scales. It had been green and brown. Now he had thick muscles, and his skin was a tannish color. Before, his mouth had been deteriorated to the point of nothingness. Now he had a full mouth of teeth, a pure white and beautiful smile. Now he was young and alive. *So alive.*

"YOU!" I screamed. "You did this to me! Here, take this back! I don't want it anymore."

The man laughed. "Oh, this is only the beginning, boy. I'm afraid you haven't seen the worst of it yet."

"The worst of it? What do you mean?" I responded.

"Tell me, boy. Does your head hurt?" It felt like the man could read my thoughts. Like he knew what was happening inside me.

"Yes, and it's getting worse. My head is pounding," I said.

"Yes, I see. Tell me this, boy. Have you tried to rid yourself of the phone? Have you tried to rid yourself of Ghost*?"* The man was no longer laughing. He had a serious tone in his voice.

He knew about Ghost. *What is happening?*

"Yes, I tried to throw it out yesterday, but then it showed back up on my dresser later," I said.

"You're only making it worse!" the man said. "It makes him angrier when you do that. It speeds up the process."

"What do you mean? What is happening to me? What process?" I said.

The man looked me up and down. He walked in circles around me. I was crying again now.

"Boy," he said. "Lift up your shirt."

"No!" I screamed. "Why should I—"

"DO IT!" the man shouted, cutting me off.

I didn't want to, but I obliged and lifted my shirt. To my horror, my stomach looked even worse now. There were brown and green scales and slime everywhere. My body looked like a skeleton, all skin and bones. Several tiny, thin moles speckled my skin, which looked like it had aged a hundred years overnight. I wanted to puke. I could barely stay upright.

"Do you see now, boy? You are in grave danger!" The man stared directly into my eyes as he spoke. He didn't blink, he didn't move.

I wanted to look right back at him, but my eyes filled with tears. My head was pounding, and I couldn't concentrate for even one second to get my thoughts straight. I needed to think logically, but none of this made any sense.

I straightened up and tried to regain my composure.

"What is happening to me? Tell me everything you know," I begged.

"There are forces in this world greater than your

little mind can comprehend, boy. That cell phone contains spirits from beyond."

My mind was racing, trying to comprehend what the man was talking about. *Spirits? As in ghosts?* And my mind immediately raced back to all the messages and videos. They were all sent or uploaded by Ghost.

"So you mean to tell me that this phone belongs to a ghost? A spirit?" I asked.

The man responded with a serious tone in his voice. "I'm afraid I don't know who this phone 'belongs' to, boy. But I do know that the horrors in that phone are hungry. They are always hungry, and they are always looking to feed."

I wiped a tear from my eye, grasping for my own thoughts. The man continued.

"And unfortunately for you, boy, your essence, your lifeforce, is what they want. Your soul is their next meal!" The man had lost his composure and was yelling at me now.

My chin trembled. I didn't understand. None of it made any sense! My essence? My lifeforce?

He continued. "They will not stop until there is nothing left of you! And then they will find another poor human to feed off of. And then another, and another. And so it will go on and on"—the man paused, staring off into the woods—"and on."

I looked down at the phone in my hand. None of this was real. None of this was actually happening. In a moment, I was going to wake up and be back in my bed. Buttons would be licking my face, and I would head out to meet Brad.

"How do I beat it?" I was gasping for air as I spoke. "How do I beat this spirit?"

The man looked through me now, his stare ice cold. "Beat it? Oh, my dear boy, you can't beat it," he said.

I didn't believe him. "What do you mean, I can't beat it?" I cried out.

"You cannot beat the spirits in that phone," he said. "You cannot win."

"But you did!" I yelled directly at him.

"Boy, I did not beat anything. I simply passed it on."

This was all just one big joke. Just one giant joke. Any minute, my friends would come out of the woods and laugh at me. I would no longer be alone, no longer be afraid. It would all be just one big goof.

But of course, that didn't happen. All of this was real. And if I didn't figure out what to do, I was going to end up looking like that man had. Even worse, I was going to end up … dead.

Chapter 16

I took the phone out of my pocket. I looked at it with fright, but also with fascination.

None of this could truly be my reality, but it was. I didn't know how or why this was happening to me. But I did know that if I didn't do something quickly, things were going to get much, much worse.

I stared down into the black abyss of the screen. It was so dark. Then the screen lit up with several messages, coming in moments apart. They all said the same thing.

Join us down here in the dark. We are so hungry.
Join us down here in the dark. We are so hungry.
Join us down here in the dark. We are so hungry.
Join us down here in the dark. We are so hungry.

I pulled myself together and looked up, but the man was gone.

"Hey! Where did you go?" I called out.

But the man was nowhere around me. The woods had become a lonely circle of sadness. My phone and I were all by ourselves. I put it into my pocket and ran.

I moved quickly out of the park, navigating around the trees and bushes. My head throbbed as I ran. The reality of my headache came crashing down on me in that moment. My head hurt because a spirit from beyond—a *ghost*—was slowly stealing my essence, slowly stealing my body, slowly stealing my soul. And it hurt.

I *felt* the change now. I didn't know if it was because I was now aware of my condition or if it was simply getting worse by the second, but I felt my stomach turning in knots. It was horrible. These were not normal pains. I felt weakened, as if my body were being sucked away through an invisible vacuum. Most importantly, it felt like my mind was turning to mush, one brain cell at a time. I needed to act fast, or I wouldn't be coherent enough to do anything about it.

I walked into my house quietly. I needed to fix this, but I could barely think straight. My head was spinning now, and I was walking crookedly. I slowly made my way up the stairs, one step at a time. Step … by step … by step. Each one took longer than the last. I slowly entered my room. I was just able to make out Buttons, but my vision was completely blurry. I fell onto my bed.

I woke to a voice. *"Jesssssieee ..."* it said. "Come join us, Jessie!" Every syllable was drawn out longer than any human would ever do. My body froze.

"Down here, Jessie. We are hungryyy, pleaseee joiiinnn usss."

I was frozen and exhausted, but with the only ounce of strength I could muster, I picked myself up out of bed and made my way toward the sound.

"Hello?" I said.

There was no response, though.

"Who's there?" I made it to the staircase before anyone or anything responded.

"Down heeeeere, Jessie. Just a little bit farrrther. You're almost therrrrrre."

The voice was getting louder, so I knew I was getting closer. I wanted to stay as far away from it as possible, but something was pulling me toward it. It was like I couldn't control my actions. My feet were moving without my mind agreeing to do so.

"Mom?! Dad?!" I called out.

They had to come help me. Had to! I waited, and I prayed for their response. I needed someone to help me.

"Please, Mom! Please, Dad! Help me!" I yelled.

The only thing that spoke back was the evil spirit.

"We are all alone down here, Jessssieee. We need a neww friennnnd, and we are so very hungryyy," it hissed.

I finally stepped off the staircase. Walking down felt like it had taken forever. The pull was getting even stronger now.

I was frightened, more than ever before, but for some reason, I felt good. Something in me *wanted* to go toward the spirit. No, something in me *needed* to go toward the spirit. And my body didn't feel bad, as it had before. My head felt great. I felt better than good. I felt strong and ... *hungry*. What I wanted and needed was radiating from the voice calling to me. Just a few steps farther and I would be satisfied. My thirst would be quenched.

I took several more steps. I was just able to make out a bright white light coming from the kitchen. My hunger was larger than ever now, my thirst so big it felt unable to be satisfied. My stomach was twisting in desire, and my tongue was dry to the touch. But this all felt deliciously good. I was tingling with excitement. But also, I felt cold. Deep down inside, there was a coldness that was spreading through my body. I knew there was something wrong. I suddenly realized my hunger was not a good thing. I was not craving food or drink. I was craving something else. Something *worse*. These cravings were pure evil.

I took my final steps toward the light and entered the kitchen. There was a figure in the brightest part of the room. I was just able to see the outline of him. His back was toward me.

"What do you want?" I asked.

The glowing outline was that of a young boy. He stood turned around but did not say anything. I no longer felt cold but *freezing*. It was like my *essence* was cold. Not just my outsides, but my insides. Everywhere was shivering. I was now within a few feet of the glowing outline of the boy.

Finally, it spoke.

"What do we want?" it hissed, sounding like surround sound in my ears.

Even though there was only one person standing in front of me, it still referred to itself as "we."

It continued. *"We want you, Jessie."* And the spirit turned around. Except it wasn't a spirit at all.

It took me several moments before I realized what I was staring at. I was in disbelief, but I was staring at myself. At the same time, it wasn't me at all. It shared most of my features, but it was not complete. It was translucent and pale. It was me as a spirit.

The spirit version of me reached out and grabbed my wrist, and I immediately felt a wetness on my face.

Buttons was licking my face. He was slobbering everywhere. I was lying in my bed. It was a dream.

"Oh, Buttons. I love you, buddy. Thank you."

I was happy to make it out of the dream alive, but I knew that I needed to do something now, or the next time, I wouldn't be so lucky.

Chapter 17

I didn't know what to do. I had all kinds of scenarios running through my mind. All of them ended with me getting taken by Ghost. I needed to come up with a plan. Something, anything. I wished my head didn't hurt so much.

I picked up the phone and started looking through it. If I was going to come up with a plan, I needed to know what I was dealing with. I looked at the pictures, the contacts, the web browser. I thought maybe there could be a clue, something that could give me some information on how to stop this thing. This spirit. But there was nothing.

And then my phone buzzed. Pain shot through my body as it did. It was a text message from Josh. Why was Josh texting me? I didn't have time for this. It read:

Can we talk?

I wasn't sure why he wanted to talk, but maybe if I explained to him what was actually happening, he would be able to help. Any ally would be huge.

I'll meet you on 86th St. in ten minutes, I replied.

When I arrived to meet Josh, he had his hood up and was looking down at the ground. He must have heard my footsteps, because he spoke before I was even close to him.

"How did you get that video, man?" Josh said.

That was a good question. The only way I could think to respond was by telling the truth.

"What I'm about to tell you is not going to make any sense, but I need you to believe me, Josh," I said.

He looked up at me. "Believe you? You humiliated me in front of everyone at school. In my own home!"

I didn't have time for his sob story. "Look, Josh, I get it. I know you're angry, and I'm sorry. But I need you to listen to me right now and believe the words that come out of my mouth," I pleaded.

"Hey, you don't look so good, Davidson," Josh declared.

"Yeah, I know. That's why I need you to listen to me. I'm in trouble and I need your help." Josh looked at me expectantly. "My phone is alive," I said.

Josh continued to stare at me for a moment, then turned and began walking away.

I ran up to him and grabbed the back of his shirt. "Please," I said.

Josh looked into my eyes. "Your face," he

whispered. "What's wrong with your face?"

The change must have been spreading. It must have been getting worse.

"I'd never even seen that video. My phone found it on its own. There is something evil inside my phone, and it's slowly taking over my soul." I paused before continuing. "And if you don't help me, I may not make it."

I did my best to give Josh a quick rundown of my story. The man, the phone, @Ghost, my dream, everything. Josh pushed my hand off his shirt but didn't look away for a second. "You're being serious, aren't you?"

I nodded, knowing Josh definitely still had his doubts.

"Well, how am I supposed to help?" he asked sarcastically.

"I don't know, have you ever seen any horror movies? Anything that might help me?" I could see that Josh was trying to use his brain, trying to think of anything that might help, but I still wasn't sure he believed me.

"Of course, but I don't know how that would help you. This is real life!" Josh said.

The two of us were quiet for a few minutes before Josh spoke again.

"Usually in horror movies, the main character needs to go back to the root of the problem somehow. Then they find some clue that can help them solve it. Have you tried that?" Josh said.

I'd already gone to see the man who was responsible for all of this, but it hadn't been any help.

"Yes," I responded. "Remember that video Brad posted of the weird guy in the hood?"

"Yeah, that was insane!" Josh laughed.

I punched him in the shoulder. This was nothing to laugh at. "I think that's what's happening to me! That guy is the reason for all of this. He was the one who gave me the phone," I said.

After another minute, though, I realized Josh was right. If I was going to actually solve the problem, I needed to go back to the root of it all. And the person who was there with me when it started was Brad.

"Come on," I said, dragging Josh along with me as we headed over to Brad's apartment.

Once we were outside, I went to call him from my phone, then thought, *Better not.* Using the phone might speed up the process. It might be painful.

"Call him," I said to Josh.

"What?" Josh replied.

"Call Brad." So Josh did.

Brad had no idea why Josh Hartley was calling him in the middle of the night, but nonetheless, he answered, and he joined us on the street in a moment's time.

"This better be good," he said. "And why are the two of you together right now? I thought you kicked him out of your house, Josh."

I jumped in. "Listen, there's very little time to explain."

"Dude, you look terrible." Brad had the same reaction that Josh did when he saw my face. I didn't want to know what I looked like. It gave me the chills to think about it.

"You were there with me," I said.

"What? I was where with who?" Brad responded.

"You were there that first day we saw the man, don't you remember?" I waited for Brad's nod, then continued.

"That man gave me this phone. Before he gave it to me, we saw him on the street together. He looked directly at me and whispered my name. He knew who I was. Remember?" I said.

"Yeah, but so what? What does that have to do with any of this? How does that creep knowing your name help you in your current condition?" Brad said urgently.

"There needs to be a reason for all of this. How did he know who I was? He must have been watching me for days, or even weeks. Maybe even months or years!" I cried out. "He was watching me for a reason. He scouted me. He knew I was the perfect person to give this phone to."

"Yeah, but he could have just thrown it away. Why did he want to give it to you instead of getting rid of it?" Josh asked.

"I told you—I tried to get rid of the phone once. I threw it in the garbage can on 86th Street. It showed back up on my dresser the next day. The man said something about not doing that again. He mentioned that it 'makes him angry'," I said.

"Wait, what did you just say, Jess?" Brad asked.

"I said that it makes him angry."

"No, before that. You said the man knew your name, that he was scouting you. When he gave you that phone, you didn't just take it, right?" Brad was on to something.

"Correct. Before he gave me the phone, he made me promise him something," I replied. And the memory came flooding back to me. We were standing in the heart of the park. Everything around us was dark except for the dim lanterns lighting up the man and his rug.

"Promise that you'll accept this gift from me, this cell phone. It's yours forever. But you may never return it. You must keep it, and you may never give it back to me."

As I went through my story again, both Josh and Brad paid close attention. They were transfixed by each syllable that came out of my mouth.

"That's it!" Brad cried out. "You can't get rid of the phone—it only makes him angrier!"

I was confused. I knew that already. Throwing away the phone had only made things worse. I'd found that out the hard way.

Brad continued, "You said that he knew your name, and that you aren't able to get rid of the phone no matter how hard you try. But somehow, the man was able to get rid of the phone. He got rid of it by passing it along to you, right? He didn't get rid of it, he gave it away!" Brad smiled.

I thought I understood what Brad was saying, but I didn't like it.

"So what you're saying is that in order to break this curse, I can't just get rid of the phone. I can't smash it to pieces or throw it away. I need to pass the phone along to someone else?" I said.

"That's exactly what I'm saying." Brad puffed his out chest as he spoke. He knew he had done well.

Josh chimed in. "But doesn't that mean this spirit will haunt whoever you give it to?" Both Josh and Brad took several steps away.

I thought long and hard, trying to process everything they were saying. This had to be it. This was the answer. I couldn't get rid of the phone; I needed to give it to someone else to lift the curse and let Ghost feed off of them. His hunger needed to be fulfilled one way or another.

The three of us stood there as reality came crashing down on me. My headache was worse than it had ever been. I was having trouble seeing and I couldn't think straight. The sun was beginning to rise all around us. The sunlight was splitting my head open.

"Dude, we have school in, like, two hours," Brad said. "My parents have no idea I'm gone."

"Neither do mine," Josh replied.

"Neither do mine. Not like it matters, anyway. These

are my final hours on this earth. If I can't pass this thing along to someone else, it will finish the job. I'm a goner," I said.

Brad immediately tried to relax me. "Dude, we're going to figure this out, everything's going to be—"

I interrupted Brad. "Wait, that's it. THAT IS IT! Brad, you are a genius!" I gave him a big kiss on the cheek with my skeleton lips.

Brad and Josh were both confused. "What are you talking about?" Brad asked.

"School starts in two hours! Grab Sara and meet me at the normal spot!" I yelled back at them excitedly. And with those words, I went home to Buttons and crawled back into my bed, hopefully not for the last time.

Chapter 18

I didn't wake up to Buttons licking my face. Buttons was lying in the corner of the room. He wanted nothing to do with me. He just lay on his belly and stared. He must have been scared of my appearance.

I picked myself up out of bed. My head, neck and back hurt. I had aches and pains everywhere. My vision was blurred, and I could barely walk straight. If this plan didn't work, I was done for.

I grabbed my schoolbag, packed everything, including my cell phone, and said goodbye to Buttons.

"I love you, Butts. If I don't come back today, just know you were the best dog I could ask for." I tried to kiss him on the nose, but he pulled away in fright.

On my way out of my room, I caught a glance of what I looked like in the mirror. I was grotesque. My skin was a thin, green spider web stretched out across my body. I had green pus and ooze jutting out everywhere. My head was completely bald except for a tuft of hair on each side. My mouth was thin and wiry. My lips were practically gone. Who was this skeleton staring back at me? I had to look away. The process must have sped up significantly overnight. Ghost knew what I was up to. He was trying to finish me off.

I couldn't go out like this. I waddled over to my closet and put on a dark hoodie. I covered up all my visible skin, made my way down the stairs, and almost managed to creep out my front door before Dad called out to me.

"Hey, squirt! How'd you sleep last night!?" he said.

"Late for school, Dad. Gotta go!" I said, walking out the front door.

I left to meet Brad, Sara, and Josh.

They were in position exactly where I asked them to be. I walked up with my hood pulled down low and spoke.

"Here's the plan." I went over it with them start to finish. If this was going to work, I needed all hands on deck. This was life or death. I couldn't risk anything going wrong.

"Is everyone good?" I made sure one last time before what might be my final trip to school.

We all put our hands in the center, although my hand didn't look much like one anymore. They were half the size they'd been and were shriveled to prunes. I grabbed my heavy gloves from my jacket pocket and put them on.

We made our way along our normal route. "Ey, boys!" Geno called out to us. "No breakfast today?"

"Not today, Geno!" Brad called back. "Super late, gotta go!"

"Ey, who's the small fry?" Geno was referring to me, of course. He must not have realized it was me underneath the hood, jacket, and gloves.

We entered school for what I feared might be my last time. The nerves grew in my body. If it hadn't felt real before, it did now. This was it, my moment of life or death. If this didn't work, I would be done for within hours.

Everything seemed so routine, so normal. Everyone was at their lockers, as always. But none of them knew what was going on. The four of us walked side by side through the halls, taking it all in. The man, the phone, the videos, my appearance, the plan—everything had come down to this one moment. None of us even bothered to grab our books; none of that was important now. It all seemed so inconsequential in that moment, to be honest. Schoolbooks? Who needs 'em, anyway!

Sara went into Mr. Miller's class first. She began her part of the plan.

"Good morning, Mr. Miller! Beautiful Monday, don't you think?" She stood on the other side of his desk to distract him from us entering the room. I couldn't let Miller see what I looked like under my hood. It would ruin the whole plan. He would think I was some kind of monster! Sara kept going, but Miller just stared back at her.

"I'm really looking forward to that test on Friday, Mr. Miller." Again, Miller stared up at her but said nothing.

Brad and Josh helped me to the back of the room while Miller's attention was fixed on Sara. It was difficult for me to walk even a short distance. The trek to school had sapped every ounce of energy I had left. I stood with my back toward Miller the Killer. Josh and Brad left me to go to their seats. They sat down quickly and motioned for Sara to do the same.

"Well, all right, Mr. Miller. Time for class!" Sara said. She went to her seat and sat down. She quickly glanced at me in the back of the room to make sure all had gone according to plan. It had.

"All right, class. Time for us to begi—" Miller stopped. He didn't finish his sentence, because something in the back of the room had distracted him. That something was me.

I took one long deep breath, pulled my cell phone out of my pocket, and held it up to my ear. I pretended to be on a call.

"Mr. Davidson, is that you? It must be, given that yours is the only seat not filled at the moment," Miller the Killer said.

I didn't respond.

I could sense the anger growing in Miller. His face

boiled red, his eyes watering with hatred.

"Do you have a death wish, Mr. Davidson?" His voice was getting louder. "DO YOU HEAR ME, YOUNG MAN?!" Mr. Miller was shouting now. His frustration was clear. "SIT DOWN AND GIVE ME THAT CELL PHONE, YOUNG MAN!"

I continued to hold the phone to my ear with my back facing him, ignoring his wishes.

"I WANT THAT PHONE! GIVE ME THAT PHONE, BOY!" I heard the footsteps now. Miller was walking over to me, and in a whoosh of exhilaration, he snatched the phone out of my hand.

An unbelievable sensation came over me. I could feel my body growing back to its normal size, my skin loosening over my body. The boils bursting away to nothing. My skin clearing up everywhere. I felt the hair on my head regrow within seconds underneath my hood. It had worked. My plan had worked!

"NOW TAKE OFF THAT HOOD AND SIT DOWN," Miller screeched.

I took off my hood and looked over at my friends. All three of them smiled back. We had done it. I was back to normal. I had reversed the curse and given it to Miller the Killer.

Chapter 19

After class, Sara, Josh, and Brad met me at my locker.

"Dude, we did it!" Brad said and gave me a huge hug.

"It's nice to have you back to your old self," Sara said. "I guess." We all laughed as she, too, gave me a hug.

"Listen, I know I was kind of a jerk to you, Davidson, but you're a good dude. Friends?" I was shocked to hear those words from Josh.

"Friends," I said. And the four of us engaged in a group hug at our lockers and went on to second period.

The rest of the day was easy. I thought constantly about the phone and how scary and real it all was. I was just glad it was over.

Brad met me at the end of the day, as he always did. We walked home along our normal route.

"Hey, Geno!" I said. "We're sorry about this morning, but we were in a rush!"

"Ey, no problem, gentleman! You are looking better, Jess-man! I'll catch you guys tomorrow, same time, same place!" Geno fist-bumped us both, and we were on our way.

We reached the point where we always split up, and Brad said to me, "Hey, do you think it's wrong, what we did?"

I thought for a moment before responding.

"Ya know, this whole time, all I wanted was a cell phone. I just wanted to be part of the group, part of everything. I felt so alone. I felt left out." I stood for a minute before continuing. I let the wind flow through my full, thick head of hair. I let the breeze touch my skin. It was chilly, but it felt so good.

"We didn't doom Miller. That phone will suck him dry, but it will give him a choice. When it comes time, he will make it," I said.

And with that, Brad and I split up and went our separate directions.

"I will tell you this, though," I called out to Brad. "One thing is for sure—I don't *ever* want to see another cell phone for as long as I live."

Chapter 20

I walked into my house. "Mom? Dad? Are you guys home?"

"Yeah, squirt! In here, come on in!" my dad called to me from the kitchen.

I made my way over to them and immediately gave them both big hugs. "Well, what's that for?" Mom asked.

"I just love you guys, that's all. And I'm sorry for giving you a hard time about the cell phone. I'm over it," I said.

Mom and Dad looked at each other. They had a peculiar look on their faces. They were confused.

"Oh, well, isn't that something. Are you sure you're over it?" Mom asked.

Dad chimed in, "Yeah, squirt, are you sure?"

Mom and Dad exchanged another look before Dad

continued talking. "Mom and I have been talking, and … well … we got you a little something!"

Dad pulled out a box from his bag. On the table, staring right up at me, was a brand-new cell phone.

Chapter 21

Mr. Jonathan Miller—the Killer, as they called him—was sitting at his desk grading papers after school. He had many thoughts running through his mind, mostly about the misbehavior of his students that day.

"The nerve of Allan Ross to have called out during fifth period today. These kids today don't know how to act. The disrespect!" Miller spoke out loud to himself. "One of these days, I'm going to lose my coo—"

Before he could finish his thought, a buzz came from inside his desk. He opened his drawer to see one of the cell phones he had confiscated earlier that day vibrating. It was a text message. He looked closer to see.

The message was clear, but it seemed to have come from no number at all. The sender's name was simple.

It was *Ghost*.

Afterword

As a middle school teacher, I am constantly in awe of the relationship between children and their cell phones! Most children are closer with their phones than any of their friends. It's become quite problematic. I've had students who cannot fathom more than moments at a time without their precious cell phones by their side. The need to check social media and be involved in the latest viral craze has become quite an epidemic. I wrote a story about one boy who so badly wanted to be part of the wave. However, his desire for a cell phone becomes an experience he will never, ever forget. I'm inspired by the way young children interact with technology and social media, and think it is quite a frightening scene in 2020. I think there are endless scares to be had with modern day technology, and many books to be written.

Growing up a *Goosebumps* mega-fan (not much has

changed), I always loved the 90's style scares like the inanimate object coming to life, or parents that never believed their children. I was enamored by the major tropes and themes like be careful what you wish for or things are not always as they appear to be. These things haven't changed! They ring truer now more than ever, only through our new vices, technology. Phones, television, music and video games affect us in special ways, but also in ways that are scary. My goal in writing this book was to take some of those same 90's scares that I grew up loving, but bring them into a new age with technology for the kids feeling alone in 2020. The kid sitting alone at home with nothing to do but read social media, or the kid at home who can't find anybody to party up with on his Xbox. The content and technology have changed, but the scares, the feeling of being alone has never been more alive.

Just a few major shoutouts here. Of course, my family. Thank you for everything Mom, Dad and Maxi. I had a picture-perfect childhood. My family allowed and encouraged me the freedom to be who I wanted to be. To hang up my *Halloween* and *Friday the 13th* posters and to play *The Legend of Zelda: Ocarina of Time* for endless hours on end before and after school. I also would be absolutely nowhere in life without my two best buds, Zenda and Kanter. Thank you, dudes, for a lifetime of memories that has only just begun, and for NEVER having to feel alone. Lastly, a MAJOR shoutout to my artist, and author of the amazing *Kill*

River series, Cameron Roubique. From the moment we crossed paths on this project, you were nothing but class. A true professional and your work is jaw dropping. Thank you for helping bring my vision alive with your insane cover art.

- Robbie Myles, New York City, 2020

Printed in Great Britain
by Amazon